CARTEL PUBLICATIONS

PRESENTS

POISON

K.D. Harris

PUBLISHER'S NOTE:
This book is a work of fiction.
Names, characters, businesses, organizations, places, events and incidents are the product of the author's imagination or are used fictionally.
Any resemblance of actual persons, living or dead, events, or locales is entirely coincidental.

Library of Congress Control Number: 2008920203
ISBN: 0-9794931-3-3
ISBN 13: 978-0-9794931-3-7

Cover Design: Davida Baldwin www.oddballdsgn.com
Editor: Renita M. Walker www.myspace.com/hdbeditorialservices
Graphics: Davida Baldwin
Typesetting: Renita M. Walker
www.thecartelpublications.com

First Edition

Printed in the United States of America

Acknowledgements

First and foremost I want to thank God, without him in my life I am nothing.

I want to thank Ms. Charisse Washington, VP of the Cartel Publications. Thanks for believing in my work and passing it on to Ms. T. Styles, President and C.E.O of The Cartel Publications, who has helped make my dream come true.

A special thanks to Ms. Davida for the awesome cover and the cartel Pep-squad for the encouragement. Thank you to all of you who worked behind the scenes to get "Poison" ready for the book shelves.

To my fellow NA readers/authors: Thank you for pushing me to my purpose. Who would have thought a year later I would be a published author with the best Street Lit Publishing House. You're up next DnD!

To my family, J. Hall, Shelly, Lisa, Bianca, My brother John, Gina, Sheila My N.C family, Sheena, Jackie, Barbara (love ya mom) and my two favorite people in the world, my angels Tryniti and Raevyn: Thank you all for believing in me, and supporting me throughout this process. We suffered a double loss this fall; I know Aunt Monique and Grandma Lenora, as well as my father John, who was taken from us over 10 years ago, is looking down on us with a smile on their faces. Stay focused, because the race is not given to swift, nor the strong, but he that endures until the end.

My extended family: Mr. Rob & Ms. Diane, Cousin Pizzle, Tina, Neisha, Nikki, Bree, Shay, Ronnie, Kee, Rionne and Cheryl (My girl for life): You are all special to me in different ways; I love you all and thank you for being who you are. I can't forget my people's out the way; Cage 1,200, C-Mac, Fatbac, Black,T.H, Juggernaut, T.J,Biggie, Baby Boy, Heavy, Gene, My girls who were down for anything, Trina, Nae, and Nicky(I will never tell). Michele, Nicole, Lashele, Crystal, Nikki, Sherril (remember those trips down the hill) Rakee, Matt, James, A.J. We had so much fun out there back then. I want to give a shout out to Littlez, Ceo of Cash Talk Ent. Thank you for looking out. Those who I didn't name don't take it personal, blame it on my mind not my heart.

To Mr. Mann (Econ), you will always hold a special place in my heart. Just remember that I "Still believe" Love ya…

To all those who picked up this book, Thank you for supporting my dream. This is just the beginning. Stop by my myspace page and tell me what you think. www.myspace.com/author_kdharris. Thank you and I love you all….

K.D.

Dedication

This book is dedicated to my "rock" Lenora Hines; I know you're watching over me. I miss you.
4/5/1925 -9/3/2007

(A Message From The Cartel's Pep Squad Captain)

Hey Everyone!

Have you ever been a part of something so great that it almost seems unreal?

Well that's the thought that comes to mind when I think about being the Captain of The Cartel Pep Squad. Just to be able to be involved in such a progressive movement is such a good feeling. It also feels great to be connected with some of the hardest working women I know…*T. Styles, Charisse Washington, J.C. Russell* and the *Pep Squad members*. These ladies work so hard week, after week to make sure the Cartel is always shining and believe me it's not an easy task. Everyone on the entire Squad possesses the same kind of qualities that mesh us together as a family.

There are some very key characteristics that are required to even be a part of the Squad. You have to be dedicated, persistent, passionate, creative, and most of all you have to be a hustler. Bein' down for the Pep Squad requires true dedication meaning you're doin' what you can to spread the news about the Cartel regardless of what's going on in your personal life. You have to be persistent in everything you do because you'll never get anything done otherwise. Reppin' for the Squad requires for you to be passionate about the things the Cartel is doin' because if you're not passionate about it then who else will? You have to possess creativity to be down with the Squad. You have to find new and unique ways of spreading the word and you have to be able to pull some ideas from your creative side.

I think the most important characteristic that you must possess is that of bein' a hustler. Your mouthpiece must be continually turned on and you must take every opportunity and chance to promote the Cartel. Even when you don't feel like it, there's always somethin' you can do…cuz closed mouths definitely don't sell books.

It's crazy because those very same characteristics have come into play in my own life. I'm trying to make my mark in this lit game and if you're reading this and you're already in this game then you know it's not easy. In fact, it's extremely hard and let me tell you it is not for the weak. You have to be able to work hard and not fall and crack under pressure and that's also what being successful is all about. You have to be able to multitask and still maintain.

If you aren't able to get anything else from what I'm sayin' then I want you to get this…don't let anything stop you from achieving your dreams. Even if you feel that you are far off from achieving your goals, don't give up. Just take each day one day at a time and make moves toward your set goal. Don't be fooled. Success won't just come to you, you gotta be proactive and do what you gotta do and move toward it. The little steps that you take day by day will land you on the road to your success. The important thing is to take the first step.

Now, as always we must pay homage to an author we respect for his/her grind and literary journey. So it is with great respect that we pay tribute to:

Miasha

There are many things The Cartel loves about Miasha. For starters, her novels *Diary of A Mistress, Mommy's Angel, Secret Society* and *Sistah for Sale* are sure fire hits! But also, her grind is impeccable. Miasha embodies beauty, brains and talent and we love what she does.

Next it's time to rep our Squad members,

"The Cartel Publications Pep Squad"

Jessica aka "Lyric" (Squad Captain), Ms. Toya Daniels, Erica Taylor, Shawntress, Kim "Bookbabe" Gamble, Lisa aka JSQueen625, Kim aka Kariymah, Miss Tori, Essence, Ms. Jazzy.

Last but certainly not least, we want to give a shout out to our Street Team! They're growing and we appreciate everything they do.

See you at the top!
Much love,
Jessica "Lyric" Robinson aka Pep Squad Captain

Prologue

Present Day - April 1995

SPINX

-Nalyse

"I remember how we used to chill back then... smokin' a blunt and sippin' some Heineken," my baby Spinx was singing his song in falsetto. We were riding around our hood bumpin' that new *Above the Rim* soundtrack.

The heat was blazing as we rolled on the set in his new, baby blue Mercedes SL500. The Daytons on the wheels were glistening in the sun as we drifted down the street. All the skeezers were salty. They were all standing on the sidewalk in awe. My baby had his Gucci shades on, with a Lacoste polo, jean shorts, and Jordans. He was working his gansta' lean, boppin' his head to the music.

You know I was fly, too. I had on my fourteen karat gold name earrings with the onyx in the back that we just copped from Philly. My hair was laid… a French roll with a deep waved pump. I sported a white tennis skirt with a baby blue

Ralph Lauren Polo shirt.

We pulled into the middle of the circle, and the spectators crowded around us. Everybody was trippin' over the car.

"Yo, nigga, this is off the hook," someone said.

"Spinx, can I ride in ya car?" said a female.

That got my attention! I broke my neck trying to figure out who the voice belonged to. It didn't take me long to find that Meekie had her raunchy ass all up in my man's grill.

"Spinxy, baby, I know you gonna let me ride," she said in a sexy voice.

Spinx looked up at her and showed all of his pearly whites. Before he had a chance to answer I immediately shut it down.

"No baby darling." I winked. "No female besides me and Ms. Nett is riding in this car." I rolled my eyes and scooted closer to my man.

For a second the block was quiet. Until she laughed at me and said, "Little girl I ain't stuntin' you. You need to have your ass at school or riding bikes somewhere." Then she addressed my man, "Spinx, I'll see *you* later. After your little Barbie doll goes to bed." She switched her hips and walked off with the rest of her Get Fresh Crew.

She really knew how to get under my skin. I sulked and sat back in my seat. Meekie, aka Carmela Daniels, was the neighborhood ho and proud of it. All the hustlers out here usually went to her crib late at night to play cards, sleep, and screw. They thought it was a buck up because they didn't have to give her loot for any bills. She was on Section 8, got food stamps and utility checks. All they had to do was make sure her hair and gear stayed tight, and occasionally they would have the boosters hook her kids up with fresh clothes.

She used to be hot shit back in her day, but after her man got locked up in the Feds she kind of went downhill. Don't get me wrong, body wise she was still on top of her game to be thirty-two. She was brown skin, wore a Halle Berry cut, and she was small at the top and ridiculously thick from the hips down. She had a lot of these fools open.

I would hear stories when I went down the Hill to chill. They talked about how she would gargle cum and shoot that shit back out. They also talked about how she shot golf balls out her pussy and could suck a forty once bottle halfway down with no hands. Nasty, but they were fascinated. Her whole crew was like that, and me and my girls and couldn't stand them. Spinx called it jealousy, but that wasn't the case.

Meekie really gave me a hard time because I was only seventeen years old and I had snagged Spinx, aka Braxton Hayes. She had her eyes on him ever since he became the H.N.I.C. Her and every other broad out here tried hard to get with him. They tried every trick in the book, but it just didn't happen. If they did get his attention they ended up being fly by nights, nothing serious.

I had to admit, I could see why these chicks were losing it over him. He was most definitely a good catch. He had a deep dark chocolate complexion with well defined facial features. One look made you melt. He stood six feet tall and had a banging body. Milk definitely did his body good, and he was all mines. I heard that Meekie almost snagged him once. Of course that was before he laid eyes on me.

I remember when I first met him. I was twelve and had just moved to the neighborhood, and he was home from Del State for the weekend. I was watching the guys play basketball when I saw him checking me out, but I just ignored him. I mean, I was only twelve so what was a grown man hawking me for?

My new friend Keyosha, aka Kee, was like, "Oh my God!

Lyse, you see that? He's looking at you!"

I tried to play it off. "Girl what are you talking about, who?"

"Spinx! He is checking you out!" Kee said.

"What is a Spinx?" I replied.

Kee sucked her teeth. "Girl you don't know nothing. Spinx is from down the Hill. He's Spade's older brother."

Now that got my attention, I knew who Spade was. He was in the ninth grade and he was real cute. All the girls were on him. I never saw a dark skin nigga so sharp. Until I saw Spinx, that is. I darted my eyes in his direction and he waved for me to come to him. I quickly turned away but Kee didn't miss a beat, she was on it.

"Oh my God! Lyse, he wants you! Go over there! Get up and go now!"

She started grabbing on my arm and tried to pull me from the bench. I didn't want everyone to be on me so I got up and went over there.

He was surrounded by all the guys that hung on the set. My mom told me to stay away from them because they sold dope and they were no good, so I was little hesitant. Then I thought about it. My sister Kat's boyfriend was into a bunch of mess and she never said anything about him. I took a deep breath then proceeded in his direction.

"Light skin!" Spinx shouted, "Come mere, I don't bite baby."

I got a little closer.

"What's your name?" he asked.

"Nalyse," I said sheepishly. I had my head down, kicking the dirt.

"Nalyse what?" he said.

"Nyse, Nalyse Nyse." I smiled.

"Are you serious?" he asked with doubt.

"Yeah, what's wrong with that?"

"Nothing, it's cute. It has a nice sound to it, Nalyse Nyse. Like you a star or something," he joked.

That's when I noticed how nice his teeth were. *Nice smile*, I thought to myself as I laughed with him.

"So how old are you Nyse, like... fifteen... sixteen?"

I was impressed. I didn't think I looked like a teenager yet. "I'm twelve. I'll be thirteen in August," I said smiling.

His eyes widened. "Damn... you got me ready to catch a charge. Yo, Gizz." He turned around and looked at his boy. "Don't shorty look like she about sixteen? I mean, look at her bubble."

I didn't move to show him. I knew he could see it where I stood.

His boy Gizz hopped off the back of the bench and nodded. "Yeah, shorty's body is bangin'! But check it, all these young girls be lookin' like that now. It must be something in the water. Give her a few years and she'll be ready," Gizz said before he went back to counting his loot.

Spinx looked me up and down while rubbing his chin. "Well look here sweetheart… I'ma look out for you. When you get sixteen you gonna be my joint and I'ma take you to my crib down the Hill. So you keep it tight, aight?"

I had no idea what that meant but I nodded my head. He reached in his pocket and handed me a wad of cash. I took it hesitantly, but all the same.

"In case you need some lunch money or school supplies," he told me.

He reached in the car and grabbed a pen and paper. I saw him writing down his pager number and smiled. He wanted me to keep in touch with him while he was in college. I wanted to remain in contact with him as well.

Over the years Spinx continued to look out for me. When

I reached my sixteenth birthday Spinx *finally* took me down the Hill. That's when my eyes were opened to a whole new world.

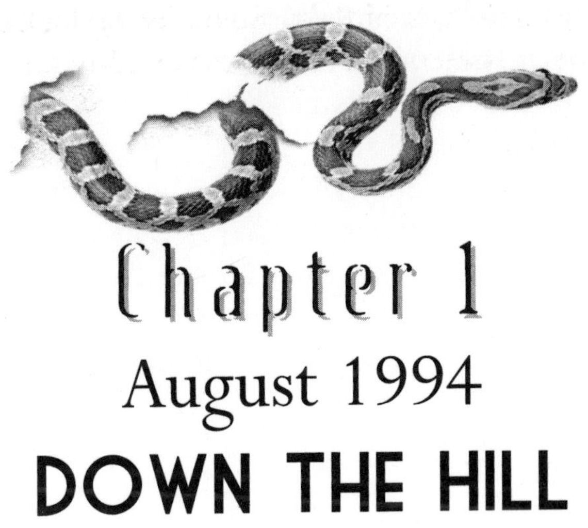

Chapter 1
August 1994
DOWN THE HILL

I couldn't believe I was finally sixteen. I was hyped! My mom woke me up bright and early that Saturday morning. She was about to work a double at the nursing home as usual. Still, she came in my room with a card and balloons.

"Hey, baby, wake up. Happy Birthday!" she said.

I pulled the covers from over my head. I was trying to act as if I was just waking up. Truth was I had just hung up the phone with Spinx. Soon as my mother left he was taking me to Six Flags. I hadn't told her about him yet and I wasn't sure if I would any time soon. My sister talked so dirty about him and the guys out here, and she would have flipped if she knew I was dealing with him.

I sat up in my bed and said, "Thanks, Ma," in a groggy tone. "What time is it?" I yawned.

"It's a little after 6 am. I have to work a double tonight and then I'm going to stay with Mr. Dave since I don't have to work tomorrow."

She looked tired. I wish she didn't have to work like that. My mother was strong. She was a single mother of three. My sister Katina, aka "Queen Kat," was the oldest. I came next and my brother Nelson, aka Stack, was last. My father was in Jersey doing whatever it is he did. We would see him on occasions, but not like that.

The reason why she worked so crazy was because she was handling most of the bills by herself. Kat's man, Rashawn, always looked out when she came up short. She refused to get state assistance because she didn't want to be a statistic. That's why we moved from the city to the burbs, or at least what we thought were the burbs. Serenity Hills was not serene at all. It used to be when we first moved down here, but like a year later it became a drug zone. People tried to sale their homes, but no one was buying so they were stuck.

What happened was the state tried this new program. You know... *let's take the people out of the city projects, give them a Section 8 voucher and move them to the suburban areas*. They thought if they changed their environment the people themselves would change. Yeah right! Alls they did was adapt and kept doing it like they knew how. Serenity Hills was the first and last development they tried that with. So we were stuck like Chuck. Now my mom knows why it was so easy for her to get a mortgage.

That's why we barely saw our mother. She had to work enough jobs to cover things. But we know she is trying to hold it down for us. So we're cool with it.

She gave me a hug and said, "I'm sorry that I couldn't give you a party or a car like your other little friends have."

I could see the sorrow in her eyes. She was so beautiful, and they said we all looked just alike. I couldn't tell. My mom, Stack and Kat had sandy brown hair and light brown eyes, and all were little a darker than me. My hair is jet black and I am a redbone, as my pop-pop used to say. I almost favored a beautiful Latina.

"So enjoy your day, sweetheart. Mr. Dave is going to take us out to dinner tomorrow to celebrate, ok?"

"Yeah, that's cool," I said. I wanted her to leave a little quicker.

She gave me another hug, yelled something at Stack and left out. I ran to my window and watched her pull out the driveway. When she was out of sight I left Spinx a message on his Sky Pager letting him know I would be ready in an hour. On my way to the bathroom I heard Kat talking to Stack. I was nosy so I wanted to know what was up.

I opened her door, and she was sitting at her vanity table looking at herself as usual. Stack was standing next to her bed. No one was allowed to sit on her sacred bed. She barely let anyone go into her room. I didn't want to be in there anyway. It made me sick. Everything was pink and lilac. She was a real girlie-girl. I stared at them both for a second. She watched me as I came in.

"Happy Birthday... jail bait," she said with a smirk.

I hated when she did that 'cuz I'm not a kid. Kat didn't like any of the guys out here at all. Especially Spinx! She told me he was a molester and that he had a real girlfriend who was grown. She said I was just the little whore he was screwing. She only said these things because her man, Rashawn Gibbs, aka Ra-Ra, was from the city and he was really running things.

Ra-Ra was only nineteen and he was already pushing crazy weight. I guess she figured nobody else could stand up to him. Kat was his girl since the eighth grade. He loved her to death and all them city bitches knew it. They thought when we moved to the Hills he would have a change of heart since its enemy territory. If you ask me, I think that just made them stronger.

I gave her the finger. "For your information, skank, I ain't give him no pussy *yet* so nobody's jail bait. He ain't got no other girl. He is always talking to me, and he's takin' me places introducing me as his young joint."

I guess I told her because she stopped brushing her hair and smiled at me. "Are you seriously retarded or something? Did you just hear what you said?"

I was puzzled.

"Never mind, you'll learn. Go have fun with *Chester-The-Child-Molester*… by the way; I got you a little setty. It's in your closet."

I ran to my room and checked the closet. I saw a bag and smiled. I quickly removed the outfit and looked at a cute little black skirt and a black and gold T-shirt that had "Prada" written across it. I looked at the skirt tag and it said the same thing. *Prada?* I thought. *What the hell is that?* I went back to Kat's room; my nose was turned up.

"What is Prada? And why didn't you buy me some Hilfiger or Nautica or something?" I said ungratefully.

Both her and Stacks laughed at me.

Stacks spoke up, "Dumb ass! That shit right there is way more exclusive than Tommy and Nautica. I'm a dude and even I know that."

Now I felt stupid. And my sister, who was sitting on the sidelines giggling, didn't make me feel any better. I could feel my face heat up from embarrassment. I stormed out of the room pissed. That's how things always went with those two. Especially Kat, she was so stuck up. She thought she was better than everybody because of her man.

All I had on my mind was getting up with Spinx. I looked at the clock and it was damn near 7:15 am, and we were leaving at 8 am. I ran the water for my shower and undressed.

I was checking myself out in the mirror. I looked at my breasts and ass. Body wise I could pass for a grown woman, including my 36C breasts. My stomach was flat as a board thanks to track. But if I had to pick, I'd have to say my ass and hips were prominent. There was no way they were going anywhere anytime soon. And to think… all of that was fitting in a junior's size 8.

I brushed my teeth, washed my face, covered my head with a pink shower cap and jumped in the shower. Once I was finished I threw on my outfit and waited by the window. A couple minutes later I heard the horn beeping outside. Anxiously, I grabbed my purse and ran to the truck.

We were riding with my best friend Kee and her man Bo. Bo was Spinx's right hand. He was a little nutso, but quiet. He had a peculiar look about him. I mean, he was cute, but something just didn't fit. Kee thought I was being mean because he was light skin. Maybe that was it, because I loved me some chocolate and he was far from it. I slid in the back with my man, and he gave me a kiss on the cheek. I said hey to everybody and then we were off.

When I turned around I saw that we had three cars following us. Spade and all the young boys and their girls were in the other cars. Bo was blasting this new CD by a group called *Bone Thugs-N-Harmony*. After five minutes I couldn't help but say they were hot. I was feeling their sound. I was all hugged up with Spinx when I saw him looking at my outfit.

"Prada?" he said with his face bunched up. "Where you get money to buy that shit? You know how much that runs?"

"My sister bought it for me. It's for my birthday." I cheesed.

He turned his head and asked, "You like that shit?"

"Yeah, I like it. It's different. No one else out here rocks it so I got to like it."

Not responding, he dug in his pocket and pulled out a lighter and a dutch. He sparked it, took a long pull and bopped his head to the music. He was silent for the rest of the ride. I couldn't help but wonder what was on his mind.

••••••••••••••••••••••••••••••••

We had a ball at Six Flags. I swear we damn near rode every ride twice. If it had been up to me I would have stuck with the water rides. It was so hot and sticky out I thought I was about to faint a few times. Everyone was coupled up so we pretty much did our own thing. Spinx won me so many stuffed animals that we had to take several trips to the truck to load them. Everything was just perfect. He treated me like a princess. I wish Kat could have seen this. Maybe she would finally see that he really loved me.

When we were leaving Kee pulled me over to the side and hugged me and said, "Happy birthday, girl! You ready to go down the Hill?"

"Yeah! I'm tryin' to see how big the house is!"

She put her hand on her hip and rolled her eyes. "Girl... it's not about being at his house, it's about what goes down inside."

I was silent as she continued.

"It's just like Meekie's house except it's real nice. His mom and brother live there too, and everyday niggas be there."

I wanted to say that the only nigga I was thinking about was Spinx, but I let her continue.

"You hear about everything that goes down there, but once you're inside you see so much shit its unreal," she said. It seemed as if her mind had drifted to the Hill.

"I'm not dumb, Kee. I can handle it," I told her.

"I know… but what you see down there stays down there.

To be honest, I'm a little shocked he's trusting you there already. 'Specially since your sister is damn near married to our arch enemy," she said switching the subject

Our? I thought. "Girl, you're being way too serious about this down the Hill thing." I laughed.

"I'm just making sure you're ready. Because once you're there, there's no turning back," she said, as she got in the front seat and shut the door.

I got in and Spinx asked me what our conversation was about. I told him she was just wishing me a happy birthday. On our way home I tried to figure out what she was talking about. She made it seem liked they killed people down there or something, and it made me nervous. Maybe I really didn't want to go *down the Hill* after all. I sat back and closed my eyes. I was getting sleepy.

Spinx whispered in my ear, "Pull your skirt up and take your panties off."

I opened my eyes and turned to him. "What?" I responded back. "Don't you see them in the front?"

"Just take them off," he demanded.

I did as he requested. I was a little scared because I didn't know what to expect. I was still a virgin, and he never asked me to do anything besides a few tongue kisses. He took my legs and placed them over his. Then he turned sideways and pulled me closer to his body. I was frantic. I didn't want to lose my virginity in the backseat of a Blazer! He gazed at my pussy for a minute then took two fingers and spread my lips apart. My heart raced. It was beating so hard I wondered if he felt it. Still on a mission, he rubbed on my clit with his thumb. I felt myself getting wet. I thought I was about to piss myself it felt so good. Too good. What was this feeling?

I felt his thumb slip into my pussy. It wasn't that bad because I got pap smears, and the doctors stuck their fingers in me all the time, but never like this. He continued to do this while adding an additional finger with each stroke. I became so wet that the fingers just started sliding in with no problem.

He started kissing on my neck and whispering that he loved me. At this point I didn't know what to do. My heart was beating faster. I thought it was going to jump out of my chest. Plus, I was tingling everywhere. I felt myself tense up when he went to unbutton his shorts. He stopped and laughed; then he pulled my panties back up. I didn't understand what was so funny, but I was relieved that my first experience wasn't going to be in the back of a truck. There was a look that spread across his face and I wondered what it meant.

A few moments later we pulled in front of Spinx's crib, around 11 pm. I couldn't wait to get out of the truck. It was filled with smoke and I was feeling woozy. I must have caught contact from all the weed smoking. When I reached for the door handle he stopped me. I faced him to see what the problem was, and a serious look spread across his face.

"Look, Nyse, you know after tonight shit is going to change. Whatever... and I really mean *whatever* you see, hear, or smell down here, stays here. You got me?" he asked.

I really didn't know what all the fuss was about, but I agreed anyway. "I got you. I can handle things, Spinx." I smiled, hoping I could. "You can trust me."

"Ok, now that we straight you can come on in."

I hopped out the car and went to the passenger side to wait for Kee. I stood there for about five minutes while Bo and Spinx were in deep convo about something. When I noticed she wasn't getting out I moved closer to the window and motioned for her to let it down. She rolled down the window and gave me the *"what the fuck do you want?"* look.

"Why ain't you getting out the car?" I asked.

She sucked her teeth. "Because I'm not going to the Hilton tonight," she said as if irritated. "Bo taking me to the Courtyard Marriott instead."

I was confused. "What? The Hilton? Who said anything about a hotel? I want to know why you ain't coming in here to chill with me on my birthday!" I was feeling some kind of way about it too.

She waved me off.

"Nyse, come on! We out," shouted Spinx.

I rolled my eyes at my so-called best friend and followed behind him, after watching the car pull off. Spinx opened the door and the house was filled with smoke. I tried to wave some of it from my face, but it was too thick. I looked around and from what I could see the house was sharp. The living room was painted a deep cranberry color with accents of gold. A matching leather furniture set and gold mirrored tables dressed the space. I noticed the gold coffee table had a glass bottom with an aquarium. I expected to see fish; instead there was a big ass nasty snake. A few guys that hustled for Spinx were playing Super Nintendo on the fifty-two inch TV.

He led me into the dining room where his mom, aka Ms. Nett, had a card game going on. They were cussin', fussin' and drinkin'. Ms. Nett was yelling across the table at some lady about her cheating. The lady got up and told Ms. Nett she better sit her drunken ass down before she whipped her ass. Ms. Nett snatched the lady up from across the table and flicked a blade from out of her mouth.

"What you say, bitch?!" yelled Ms. Nett. "I'll carve your mutha fucken face like it's Thanksgiving!"

I tugged Spinx's arm and whispered for him to do something. He just laughed and said that shit happened every weekend. The woman was still talking cash shit to Ms. Nett. Finally the woman pulled the cards that she was hiding out, and Ms. Nett let her go. She looked at us and walked over.

Ms. Nett was a big woman. She was real pretty, with smooth chocolate skin. She hardly looked old enough to be Spinx's mom.

"Wassup, Nett?" Spinx said.

I couldn't believe he just called his mom by her name. She gave him a pound and looked me up and down.

"So, I see you finally got your happy young ass down here."

I didn't know if she was being sarcastic or not so I just smiled.

Spinx grinned. "Stop trippin', Nett. You scarin' her," he said.

She smirked and replied, "I don't want no shit out of her. You hear, Braxton?" she said, pointing her finger in his face. "I told you her ass is still a baby, and your old grown ass is twenty-two! You can get locked the fuck up chasing some young pussy." She looked me over again and said, "But I have to admit, she is cute. She got a nice little shape on her too." She leaned over to me. "Don't go and get knocked up. Your ass will spread across the country like mine did."

With that she went back to control her card game. We were heading towards the stairs and she yelled, "You clean your own bloody sheets when you're done."

Spinx bagged up laughing. I was totally embarrassed.

We went upstairs to his room, but before we got there I heard all this deep moaning and bed squeaking. Spinx paused before going in his room and opened the door across the hall where all the noise was coming from. Spade was in the room, and he was pounding away at some chick. Sweat ran down his back, and the girl's legs were opened like a pair of scissors. Who ever the chick was, it was not his girlfriend Vanessa. I stood there in shock and Spinx moved in unnoticed. Spade made it known by his actions that door wide open or not, he wasn't stopping his flow.

Spinx walked back out of the room with some incense and shut the door behind him. He gently grabbed my hand for me to follow.

His bedroom was nice. He had a king sized black lacquer bedroom set, and there were mirrors on the headboard. Matter of fact, there were mirrors everywhere in the room. I stood there looking around while he busied himself with a pack of White Owls.

He patted the side of the bed. "Get comfortable."

I timidly made my way over to him.

He turned his light on. It was blue and it made the room look real nice. He cracked the Owl open and emptied it in the ashtray. He then filled it with some weed. I sat there not knowing what to do. He lit it, took a few puffs and passed it to me.

"I thought you said you didn't want me smokin' this stuff," I said nervously.

He nodded. "Yeah, I did. But you can smoke with me though, I can protect you." He took another hit and passed it my way.

I tried to inhale and started to cough out of control.

He laughed.

I smiled.

"Slow down, Nyse…. Take your time."

He showed me how to do it, and three blunts later you would have thought I was a pro at it. I was feeling loose by then. No longer nervous, I lay on the bed cheesing. I was so messed up that I didn't realize that I was in just my bra and panties. *When did he undress me?* I thought.

Spinx had also stripped down to his boxers and was messing with the radio. He popped a tape in and came back to the bed with me. He climbed on top of me and kissed me. Then the song "*Just Me and You*" by *Toni! Tony! Tone!* came on. He started kissing on me and sucking on my nipples. I just lay there enjoying it all. This was going to be the night I would lose my virginity, I knew it. He unsnapped my bra and engulfed each breast in his mouth. My panties were soaking wet. He must have read my mind, because he reached down and slid them off.

He began rubbing between my legs and whispered, "You ready to be my woman, Nyse?"

"Yes," I moaned.

"You sure?"

"Yes," I said flatly, although anxious.

He got off the bed and pulled off his boxers. That's when fear set in. I came face to face with his big fat pole. My eyes nearly popped out of my head. He took my hand and ran it up and down it. He told me to not be afraid because it was my friend, and friends don't hurt you, they make you feel good.

He got back on the bed and opened my legs. To my surprise I was really relaxed. He pulled me closer to him and I felt my leg begin to shake. He leaned over and kissed me and said it's gonna be all right. He rubbed the head of his dick against my opening and slowly inched his way in. It wasn't that bad, until after a while, when he forced the rest of himself in me. I felt something rip. I screamed and tears fell from my eyes.

He kissed me and told me not to cry, the worst was over. My insides were stinging for a while, but eventually it did get better. Matter of fact, I loved it. *Silk's "Loose Control"* was playing now and that's exactly what was happening. I was losing control. Things were happening that I never felt before. My pussy seemed to have a mind of its own. Weird feelings were coming back to back. *Am I having an orgasm?*

I wondered.

Spinx really got into it and started to speed up. I could feel his dick inside of me swelling. Then, something happened that I couldn't explain. All this stuff came flowing out of him and into me. I thought he pissed inside of me. Afterwards, I lay in his arms trembling all over with excitement. He gave me a tight squeeze.

"Are you ok?"

I couldn't speak. I gave a quick nod.

"You officially belong to me. You better not neva, eva, give yourself to another nigga. I love you girl." He gave me a kiss on the lips and rolled off the bed.

I finally managed to pull myself up. All of a sudden I felt shy. I pulled the sheets up to my neck and whispered, "I love you too."

He smiled. "I know you do, Nyse." He put his boxers on and disappeared into the bathroom.

Although my coochie was throbbing with pain, I managed to put a smile on my face. I was finally Spinx's woman. My throat was a little dry. I looked at the nightstand on my left and noticed that there was still a little juice left in my bottle. That's when I noticed the time. *3:15 am? It was just a little after 2:50 am when we started*, I thought. I shrugged my shoulders. What seemed like an eternity was just a matter of minutes.

I took a sip of the juice. I got up and switch on the regular lights. Once the lights were on I noticed myself in the mirror. I dropped the blood soaked sheet from around my body and screamed.

Spinx came running out of the bathroom. "What's wrong?" he asked. He looked at the sheet lying on the floor.

I pointed at the sheet. "Why… why is there so much blood? It's too much, isn't it?" I said fearfully. I could tell he was trying to hide his laughter.

He grabbed me by the hand and led me to the bathroom. "Baby, it's all right, those things are supposed to happen. Didn't your mom school you about this?" he asked while running the shower water.

I put my head down in shame. I didn't feel like a woman anymore I felt like a stupid little girl. The truth was I didn't know that this could happen. My mother never told me about sex. The only thing I knew was what Kat talked about, and her stories didn't come close to this experience.

"Yeah, we talked about it… I guess I just forgot." I lied.

He handed me a towel and rag. I got in the shower.

Before he left out the bathroom he said, "After you're done you better go downstairs and wash those sheets before Nett gets in that ass."

After I was done taking a shower I threw on one of his T-shirts and a pair of too big gym shorts. *The worst part is over now,* I thought. I opened the bathroom door and alls you could hear was Spinx laughing loudly with someone on the phone. I hoped that he wasn't talking about me. I felt my cheeks turn red. I hurried to the room and gathered the sheets. He smiled my way and continued running his mouth. I took the sheets to the laundry room and noticed that there were just a few people left in the house. Ms. Nett was handing my English teacher, Mr. Knotts, a bag of crack. Mr. Knotts had a huge grin on his face.

"Thanks, Ms. Nett. I'll see you later on today to show you that," he said happily.

Ms. Nett nodded and showed him out the door. I didn't know what to do. I was stunned. *Dang, Mr. Knotts gets high!* I thought. I couldn't believe it. I put the sheets in the washer and left out. Ms. Nett met me at the steps.

She stood in front of me with a stern look and seriousness

in her tone. "You know the rules, right?"

I looked her in the eyes when I answered her to let her know that I was trustworthy. I was always told if a person can't look you in the eyes then they're either up to something and can't be trusted, or insecure. I was neither of the two. "Yeah, I won't say anything."

A warm smile spread across her smooth chocolate skin. She shook her head in agreement and turned to walk up the stairs. A feeling of relief came over me. *I think she accepts me now*, I thought. Halfway up the steps she came to a stop. She turned around and looked me over and snickered.

"You look a little flushed, was Braxton too much for ya?"

I felt my face go from pale to beet red. I was totally embarrassed, but I laughed it off with her. I could see that I was gonna have to get used to her sarcastic humor.

On the way up the stairs she yelled back, "Welcome to womanhood!

Chapter 2

Present Day - April 1995

THROWING SHADE

Spinx slid coolly out the Benz to greet his fans. Everyone began to crowd around to get a closer look at the shiny blue car. The attention made Spinx beam with pride. The people in the hood made him feel like a celebrity. He tilted his shades and lightly leaned against the car. He was careful not to leave any dents or smudges. He was in his glory.

I sat in the passenger seat with a smug look, sulking over Meekie's comment. I turned my head and looked the other way, disgusted. I couldn't even pull myself together to be by my man's side. That bitch just *ruined* my day. She really knew how to make my skin boil. She wouldn't have bothered me so much if I'd never caught her sucking my man off. I saw that shit with my own two eyeballs.

A couple of months ago I was coming home from a track meet. I had on my grey and blue Wilson High Track Team jogging suit, looking cute as always. My team came in first place, and I wanted to show Spinx my trophy. I knocked on the door, but there was no answer. After turning the door knob I discovered that the door was unlocked. I went straight upstairs to our bedroom and got the surprise of my life.

The door was wide open. The first thing I saw was Spinx's bare, black ass, with his jeans around his ankles. I just stood there for about thirty seconds with my jaw dropped. I was really pissed when I noticed nasty ass Meekie on her knees slobbing on dick that belonged to me. I hauled off and threw my trophy, aiming directly at Meekie's head. Unfortunately, I missed. Instead it went crashing into several cologne bottles on the dresser. It was enough to get their attention.

"What the Fu-," Spinx noticed my reflection in the mirror and quickly snatched his dick out of her mouth. "Nyse… damn…. Yo, this ain't what you think!"

I was on fire. If I had a blade I would have cut his ass. "What the fuck you mean it ain't what I think? You got your little black dick all up in her mouth, Spinx. You can't lie… I saw it with my own eyes!" I yelled.

Meekie was still on her knees with a grimace on her face. "Look, I ain't got time for this shit. We can either handle this now, or you can stop over later and we can finish up. Either way I need my shit now." She rose from the floor and held her hand out to Spinx.

In my mind I just kept thinking no the fuck she didn't just say they could finish. "Bitch, he ain't coming to your trifling ass house to finish nothing! You better get the fuck out before I fuck your old ass up!" I snapped.

Meekie was older than me, but I was damned if she was gonna just play me like I didn't matter. She didn't even look my way. Spinx dug into his pocket and handed her a little blue bag. She took it and strutted pass me as she went out the door. I looked at Spinx in confusion.

"I told you it wasn't what you thought. She needed a hit

and ain't have no money. You act like I was making love to the bitch! You need to grow the fuck up, Nyse. You know what I do to make money for us, so get the fuck over it!" he said.

That was months ago, and it still bothered me like it was yesterday. No sorry; Nyce, I'll never do it again. Nothing.

Just as I was starting to get deep into my pity party, I noticed my girl Kee wobbling towards me in the side-mirror. She had on a pair of navy leggings, an oversized red and blue Gap T-shirt and a pair of white Reebok classics. Her hair was in her infamous rod curled weave pony tail with ocean waves in the front. I hurried and threw a smile on my face. There was no way I could let her see me upset.

That was the hard thing about being Spinx's woman. I had to make everyone out there think that everything was all beautiful, even if it wasn't. I refused for some bitch to think she even had a chance of taking my spot. It just wasn't going to happen. I was here to stay.

Kee stopped on the side of the car. She took a good look at the car and then stared me up and down before she spoke, "Hey, girl, I see you glossin' in that ride."

Her words were stale and her expression was vague. My smile faded slowly. Lately I had been a little suspicious about Kee's true feelings about me. Over the years she seemed to have distanced herself from me. At first I thought it was because she was busy playing house with Bo. I confronted her about it one day and she had the nerve to say I had changed. She said I was starting to *act* like Kat. I was a little upset that she had the audacity to say something so harsh. I was nothing like her. My sister was mean and treated people like they were beneath her. I was nothing like that. No. Not me.

I knew Kee didn't really mean that. I still believed something else was bothering her. I just didn't know what it was. I just hoped it wasn't a bit of *envy*. I loved Kee like a sister, and she was my only true friend. I would've hated to have to cut her off. I mean, she's the one who introduced me to Spinx. If it wasn't for her I wouldn't be with him to this day.

I ignored the thought and tilted my shades downward. "You see me, bitch," I said jokingly.

Silence.

I decided to change the subject. "Look at your damn belly... you look like you about to drop that load any minute," I said with enthusiasm.

Her face lit up when I spoke about the pregnancy. Kee was on her second baby. She already had a little girl named Myai by Bo; she was about seven months old. I went off on her when I found out that she was knocked again. I thought Bo was trying to trap her by keeping her barefoot and pregnant. He had a hold over her mind. She did whatever he wanted, and I didn't like it one bit.

For a minute I thought he was beating on her; when her looks began to fade. She was once a radiant black beauty, with flawless dark chocolate skin, almond shaped eyes and a sharp defined bone structure. Barbizon Modeling School material, and that was something to be proud of, especially if you were a female of color. You had to be something special for them to want you.

Last year she was offered a scholarship to their program. She was so excited, but was shot down by Bo. She was still going to go despite how he felt. Unfortunately, a few weeks before it was time for her to start she found out she was pregnant. I swear he knocked her up on purpose. This time around she dropped out of school and everything. She got a Section 8 voucher and moved into the apartments across the highway with Bo. After watching her life spiral downward, I was just happy I had never got knocked up. It wasn't like I was protecting myself or anything. I guess I was just lucky.

"So whatcha ready to get into?" I asked her.

"I'm ready to go down the Hill and drop this shit off to this fiend."

My jaw dropped. That's the type of shit I was talking about. She was in no condition to making any runs. I tried to hide my anger. "I know you ain't walking?"

She rolled her eyes and shifted her weight to the left. The oversized Guess bag was weighing her down. "How else do you think I'm supposed to get there? It ain't like you can take me!" she snapped.

I could tell in her voice that I was testing her patience. She looked exhausted. I held up my finger, as to say *wait a second*. I opened the car door and scooted pass her, bumping her stomach. I quickly apologized and walked over to Spinx, who was entertaining his adoring fans. I rubbed his shoulder and whispered in his ear softly. I was asking if we could drop Kee off down the Hill. When I was finished I gave him a pleading look while stroking his hand.

He kissed me on the cheek and whispered back, "Baby, don't you see that I'm busy right now? I'm not going anywhere and neither are you." He turned his attention back to his fans and continued his conversation like I wasn't even there.

I looked around and notice a few people staring at me like they were trying to figure out what was said. I usually didn't act out, but I was vexed. I looked over at Kee and she gave me a look as to say, *I told you so*. I took a few deep breaths. I had to get myself prepared for what I was about to do. Once I got enough nerve I jumped in front of Spinx and yelled in his face.

"Why you frontin' on my girl Kee? She's knocked by your boy and you can't take her down the Hill? That's fucked up!"

Everything went silent around me. It was so quiet that you could hear a knat piss on cotton. A sick feeling instantly came over me; I knew I had fucked up. I looked around at my surroundings. I noticed a few people snickering and a few with their hands over their mouths in awe. His cool demeanor quickly changed. His eyes widened in shock. Then it happened.

"Bitch, what the fuck you just say!?" he instantly grabbed me by the arm and led me across the street.

My stomach was doing flips. I was afraid of what he might do, but I refused to let him know it. Once we made it across the street he began to shake me like a rag doll. I tried to get him off of me, but his grip was too strong.

"Are you fucking crazy? I should slap the shit out your ass for trying to play in front of my peoples. Fuck that bitch… she got two fucking legs, she can walk."

He raised his hand like he was about to slap me. I knew better. This was just a show. He swore he would never put his hands on me. This was all an act to fluff up his ego. But little did he know I had a point to make, too. The hell if I was gonna go out like those other chicks that let niggas beat them down in the street.

"Ok, Spinx, you made your point. Your fans see that you have me in check, now get the fuck off me," I said with my teeth clenched.

He let go of my arm. I backed away from him and glared. We were both breathing heavy and staring each other down like we were in a draw. I looked across the street and noticed people whispering to one another, pointing in our direction. I was swole. First this bastard disrespected my ace, *and* he had the nerve to put his *hands* on me and call me out my name in public. I began to make my way back towards the crowd. He ran behind me trying to grab me. I pulled away and picked up my pace. I heard him in the background calling my name.

"Nyse!"

I didn't even look back.

"Yo, Nyse, you know you fuckin' hear me!"

I could tell that he was embarrassed by my blatant disrespect. But fuck him. *Alls he had to do was take us down the Hill, but no, he wanted to show out in front of his flunkies,* I thought. I walked past his peoples and flashed them my award winning smile. The hell if I was going to give them any type of satisfaction of seeing me distraught. Far as they knew I had that nigga eating out the palm of my hands. And that was the way it was going to stay.

I went over to Kee and took the Guess bag off her shoulder. She had a confused look on her face. I gave her a sneaky grin and she smiled back. I noticed a big rock sitting on the ground. I grabbed her hand so we could start our journey down the Hill. Just before we left I picked up the rock and threw it at the windshield and we ran.

Spinx was heated at this point. "Nalyse, you stupid bitch! I'm gonna kick your fucking yella ass!" he yelled.

Wow he called me by my name... he's really pissed, I thought. I laughed at him and kept it moving. He stood next to Gizz who was shaking his head trying hard not to laugh at his boy. I stopped in the middle of the path, turned slowly in his direction, smirked and gave him the finger.

I could hear people saying, "Oh shit, Nyse is crazy... oh my God!" Some people even had the nerve to laugh. I know he felt some type of way.

Later on I found out some new cat who obviously didn't know any better came out his mouth sideways and said, "Man, fuck her, Spinx. She ain't nuffin' but some young, dumb, pussy anyway." The fool thought that he was cool and tried to give Spinx some dap, like what he said about me gave him some brownie points. Little did he know he just earned himself a beat down that he would never forget.

Spinx acted like he was gonna give him a pound. As soon as he came close enough, he two pieced him, causing him to hit the ground hard. On cue the young boys commenced to stomping a mud hole in him.

I laughed when I heard the story. That's what his dumb ass gets. It didn't matter how mad Spinx got at me, no one could disrespect me or talk dirty about me. Especially not in his presence, because they were going to get dealt with.

Later that night my pager was blowing up. I lay on my bed listening to the Nine at Nine Countdown on Power 99FM. "*Weak,*" by *SWV,* was the number six song. That was my shit right there. I rolled over to my nightstand and picked up my clear pink Motorola pager. I laughed to myself. It wasn't anybody but Spinx. He left little codes saying I love you and then he hit me with the sixty-nine. *Hmphh... not tonight,* I sang to myself. I put the pager on vibrate and sat it on top of my nightstand. I grabbed my head scarf from the bottom of my antique white canopy bed and went to the bathroom to wrap my hair for school tomorrow.

I was so glad I only had a month and half of that shit to go. I would graduate in June, most likely with honors. No matter how much shit I got into with Spinx; I didn't let my grades slip. I wanted to go to a prestigious university and study law. It was always my dream to be a defense attorney like Johnny Cochran.

I talked to Spinx about going away to school, but he wasn't having it. He said I'd better carry my ass to Widener University and enroll in their law program. They had a campus in Wilmington, not far from the Concord Mall. I wasn't about to go to that school. I figured that I would most likely go to the University of Delaware, where my sister attended. I would stay for one year and then transfer to Georgetown. That would give me time to work on him and save some money.

I tied the scarf tightly around my head and then turned on the water to brush my teeth. In the midst of brushing I heard my mom laughing and talking to someone downstairs. I quickly turned the water off and stood quietly, trying to eaves drop on her conversation. I heard Kat's whiny voice complaining about something. I rolled my eyes and shook my head.

"Why is this chick here?" I sighed.

I didn't feel like dealing with her ass, so I was going to go to bed. Then I thought about it, she always found ways to try and make me feel inadequate. I was gonna go down there and tell her about my man's new SL500. A feeling of pride came over me. I practically ran down the steps.

When I came to the last few steps I played it off like I was going to the kitchen. I floated past the den and stopped at the door. She was complaining about an oil change or something that had to do with her piece of shit car. Well, it wasn't really a piece of shit, it was 1994 Lexus GS300, but I wasn't moved by it. I came in and sat on the couch next to my mother and gave my sister a big grin.

She turned her attention from my mother and focused it on me. "What's up, trixie? Why you smiling all big?" she asked.

She crossed her legs and sat back on the love seat. She took her manicured hands and fluffed her sandy brown shoulder length hair. She wore a little black Chanel dress, with T-strap designer stiletto heels. I never understood why she dressed like that all the time. It's not like she had a job or did anything of importance. My face was frowned up and I felt my chest tighten. *She makes me sick,* I thought. I guess my mom could feel the tension. She excused herself and went into the kitchen to start dinner.

I waited until she was out of sight and whispered, "You know we got a Mercedes SL500?" I gloated.

Kat laughed at my comment like it was some type of joke. I refused to let her ruin my fun. So I continued to smile despite her negativity.

"We... who is we? Is your name on that car, and are you talking about Bank's baby blue Mercedes?" she questioned.

Banks? What did she mean by that? Spinx told me he bought that car straight off the lot, I thought. I tried not to show my confusion. "No, my name is not on the car and it doesn't have to be. And what you mean Banks Mercedes? That's not his car!" I was getting annoyed. She was really starting to piss me off and I couldn't hide it.

She stood up and folded her arms and began to pace the floor. Her heels clicked against the cherry hardwood floors. She stood in front of me looking down on me and began her usual lecture. "Damn, Nalyse. I really thought you would have learned by now. That nigga is not gettin' it like that... he runs a fucking development. He is not a boss. Now if you want to run with a thoroughbred you need to get with Brock, that nigga been on you for years. He's younger than your so called man and has more money stacked than that nigga will ever see." She shook her head in disappointment and pulled out a phone from her Chanel bag.

I guess this bitch gonna pull out her phone to rub it in my face, I thought. "Who are you calling?" I demanded.

She was standing by the window pressing numbers and peaking out the blinds. By the way she was acting you would have thought she was expecting someone.

"I'm checking my messages... if you don't mind. I can't believe you're sitting here hyped about his bootleg car. You need to ask him to get you one. You *are* ready to graduate. See where his head is at. See if he got enough to get you your own whip." She opened the blinds and lifted them and pointed to her Lexus. "You see that shit right there; parked out front? That's my shit, in my name, that Rashawn *bought me.* And I didn't even ask for it, he just did it. You betta drop that whack nigga." She shut the blinds and rolled her eyes at me. As she walked pass me I heard her whisper, "Dumb broad."

I sat there feeling stupid. I wish I had just gone to bed instead of dealing with her. My eyes were stinging and I felt a lump in my throat. "Fuck this shit," I said to myself, fighting back tears. *Who does she think she is? Even though I hate to admit it, she did have a point. Maybe I should ask for my own whip*, I thought. She had a cell phone. I didn't even have one of those. I just had my pager.

Ra-Ra did keep my sister fly and he was paying for her education. I was going to ask Spinx what his plans were for my graduation. I tried to beat the feeling of inadequacy that was submerging my mind as I walked back to my bedroom. I closed my door and turned out the light and listened to the Quiet Storm. My last thought before I drifted off to sleep was *he'll pay for my tuition. I mean, he is my man....*

Chapter 3
HATED BY MANY

It was Thursday afternoon, and I was sitting in fourth period bored as hell. Half of the students in class were either sleep or listening to their walkman. Mr. Knotts acted as if he didn't realize that nobody was paying him any mind. He stood at a world map talking some shit about the Gulf War. I was slumped over on my desk doodling in my notebook. I had no idea why they were still trying to teach us when we were leaving in a month.

I felt someone staring at me. I looked to my left and noticed Dale Mitchell basically raping me with his eyes. I noticed the huge erection bulging out of his khaki Docker pants. Dale was a cutie in his own way. He was the Senior Class President. He had soft curly hair and smooth caramel skin. I think he was mixed with something. He usually hung with the preps and kept a blonde on his arm. However, he always had eyes for me. I was probably the only black chick he would even think about being with. If I wasn't with Spinx I might have talked to him. He drove a gold Dodge Stealth and lived in Caravel Farms. To live there you had to have cash.

I smiled and thought, *I may get a little excitement out of this class after all.* I purposely knocked my purse over on the floor in the opposite direction. Mr. Mitchell was in luck today because I wore a black Ralph Lauren tennis skirt with the matching polo shirt. When I bent over the desk he got a full view of my ass and black lace thong. My ass jiggled as I adjusted myself over the chair. I took my time while picking my things up. That is, until I saw my pager light up. I grabbed it and checked the number. Yes! It was my baby.

I threw everything into my Guess bag and packed up my books. I turned around towards Dale and winked and blew him a kiss. I heard him say, "Damn." We both looked down at his pants and noticed his wet spot. He didn't even look back up. He was ashamed and he should have been. I giggled and walked to the door. I still had ten minutes left before the bell rung.

Mr. Knotts looked at me as if he had something to say. I gave him that, *I know what you did last summer look,* and he continued teaching. I had him and a few other faculty members eating out the palm of my hand. Turned out that a lot of teachers and people you least expected got high and liked young pussy. I would see them down the Hill on a regular basis. I even caught my mailman down at that Hilton getting some young snatch, and his ass was every bit of forty-five to fifty years old.

Oh, by the way, the Hilton is that room I seen young Spade waxin' that skeez bitch in when I first went down the Hill. They used that room for their side chicks or for a discreet affair, or a D.A. as they called it. That way if the chick ever wanted to call them out she couldn't describe their bedroom or some bullshit like that. I was hyped that my baby called. I needed him to give me some money because I ran out and I needed my nails filled.

When I arrived at the payphone some chick was on it.

She was busy running her mouth on the phone. I sat there for a few minutes staring her down. She continued to talk like I wasn't there and she had all damn day. I was growing impatient so I tapped her on the shoulder.

"How long are you going to be?"

She sucked her teeth and rolled her eyes.

I stepped back in awe with my mouth hanging open. *No this huzzy didn't roll them crooked eyes,* I thought. On an impulse I snatched the phone from her and pushed the button to end the call. *I don't know who the hell she thinks she is,* I thought.

I put my money in the machine and dialed the number. While I was dialing she was breathing all heavy, standing there like I was gonna apologize and give her the phone back. I leaned up against the wall and watched her. This bitch looked a mess from head to toe. She was bald headed, the little bit of hair she had was gelled to the side. She had on a pair of too big jeans with run-over classics and a loose fitting T-shirt. Her mouth was raggedy and she was cock eyed, a pure fucking mess.

She moved closer to me like she was about to do something. I was on point. I wasn't a fighter. As a matter of fact, I'd never fought a day in my life. I had no reason to. But if I had to, I knew how to defend myself. She looked like she wanted to do something. I told that bitch to jump. She said some crap and walked off. I wasn't stuntin' her ass. I picked up the phone and talked to my baby.

I put on my sexy voice for him, "Hey, baby, I'm glad you called. I really missed you… you miss me?"

He put his smooth voice on for me, "Girl, you know I do. I'm happy you finally called me back, I was beginning to worry."

I had been ignoring his calls since Sunday when he

grabbed me up.

"No need to worry, baby. I was just in my feelings… but, ummm, we need to talk. When are you getting back?"

"Your feelings, huh… you sure that's all, Nyse? You really acted up that day. If I was any other nigga I would have whooped your ass for trying to clown me like that. See, you're lucky you have someone like me. I couldn't even imagine putting marks on that beautiful face or body of yours. I love you, girl… I just wish you would stop acting like a spoiled brat, but we'll discuss that tonight when I get home. You think you'll be able to get out late night?"

Spoiled brat? Me? He was definitely tripping. I wanted so bad to cuss his ass out, but I remembered I really needed to see where his head was at concerning *my* future. I was just about to confirm our date, but I felt claustrophobic all of a sudden. I quickly turned around and noticed I was surrounded by the crooked eye chick and the rest of her Westside Girl Crew. I sucked my teeth and told Spinx about the incident with the chick and now she was back with her girls.

I wasn't worried. These chicks knew better than to start shit with me. They knew my Sister was *Queen Kat*. They knew if they even thought twice about fucking with me they were done for. They treated her and Ra-Ra like they were fucking royalty or something. I got quiet when I noticed they were *still* standing around me.

Spinx got a little concerned. "Baby, what's up, why you get quiet on me?"

I was unmoved by their presence. "Everything is cool… I guess they're admiring my beauty, because they ain't doing shit but staring at me. I know they don't see chicks that look as good as me too often, but *damn.*" I laughed.

Spinx wasn't laughing with me. "Nyse, where are those

bitches from?"

"The Westside, but they ain't gonna do shit my sis-"

I felt the phone being snatched from me. I was about to snap until I saw who it was. Faggot ass Chauncey, one of Ra-Ra's stoolies, was standing in front of me holding the phone over my head.

"Give me the fucking phone, nigga!"

I tried to reach for it, but he continued to hold it high. I tried to jump up and get it, but it wasn't working. Chauncey stood 6'4, and I was a measly 5'4. That was a huge difference. It didn't help that his arm was all long and lanky. I pushed him. He took his big ass hand, clawed my face and mushed me. I fell to the ground, but quickly rose to my feet. I felt the heat run through my veins. I was enraged.

"Mutha fucka, are you crazy? Do you know who the fuck I am?"

He laughed at me and said, "Shut the fuck up, ho! Your name don't ring no bells here. Who are you talking to anyway, your bitch ass *boyfriend*?"

The girls started to laugh as Chauncey mocked me. He put the receiver to his ear and clowned Spinx. The bell rang to change classes and everyone started to crowd around us at the booth. I felt safe, I figured he wouldn't do shit with all these people out here, but I was wrong.

"I bet this is his bitch ass right here," he said to one of his boys. He spoke into the phone, "What's up, nigga? Your little bitch think she's running shit up in this school, but I'm about to let my sharks loose on her ass." Chauncey laughed.

I heard Spinx yell something over the phone.

Chauncey tried to clown him. "Mutha fucka, you ain't ready. Matter of fact, I'm about to slap your little pride in joy right in that slick mouth of hers."

I couldn't believe what I was hearing. *I know he ain't really about to hit me,* I thought. I saw him raise his hand like he was about to back hand me. I tried to move out the way, but those bitches wouldn't move. I tried to cover my face, but it was too late. *Slap!* It felt like thunder hit the side of my fucking face. That nigga slapped the shit out of me. I tried to hit him back and that's when it started.

Those bitches jumped on me. I was trying to fight back, but I was in a no-win situation. I balled up on the floor covering my face. I was too light for a bunch of marks. I heard people trying to break it up. I tried to look around to see if anyone from the Hills was around to help. I didn't see a soul. I heard the administrators coming and everyone scattered. Mr. Scott, the Vice-Principal, tried to help me up.

"Get the fuck off of me!" I snatched away from him.

I looked around and noticed people snickering and pointing at me. I ran my hand through my hair and noticed a clump had fallen out. *Jealous Bitches,* I thought. *I figured they would fuck with my hair.*

"Do you need to see the nurse?" Mr. Scott asked.

I looked at him as if he was crazy. There was no way you would see me hurrying off to no nurse. I refused to let anyone think they hurt me. "I'm fine, Mr. Scott. I need to get to class." I picked up my stuff and tried to walk away.

Mr. Scott looked around to see if anyone was looking. He leaned in close to me and whispered, "Ms. Nyse, who did this to you? Let me help you before this get out of control. I know what type of crowd you run with, and I can't allow any gang violence in my school. Innocent students may get caught up and that won't look good on me." He pushed his glasses up on his pointy nose.

I sighed. He ain't give a fuck about those kids; he just wanted to look good. "I don't know who did it Mr. Scott, so now could you just get the fuck out of my way?"

He reluctantly moved to the side. I felt him watching me as I walked down the hall. I went to the bathroom and went straight to the mirror. The first thing I noticed besides the big ass handprint Chauncey left was a busted lip.

I smirked. "That's all they did. I expected to see a black eye and some more shit." I laughed. "They got their rocks off, now it's my turn." I wiped my lip down. Left out the bathroom and went straight to the payphone. "I got something for they ass," I said to myself.

I paged Fatal and put code one, eight, seven. I did the same for the twins Muff and Buff. Muff & Buff, aka Melenyse & Brynn Nichols, were a force to reckon with. They were my age, but went to a Vo-Tech high school. Those bitches just rumbled for the sport of it, they were always down. We were going to get those bitches back.

I noticed my pager was going off while I was on the phone. It was Spinx. I called him back and he already knew what happened. Co-Co who lived down the Hill saw the whole thing. I didn't even know she was there. Then I got pissed. *Why ain't that bitch help me?* I thought. Spinx explained that there were too many people in her way, and by time she got through they were breaking us up. *That scandalous ass ho*! I thought. I couldn't believe she sat and watched me get jumped on. I already had it in my mind she was going to get dealt with, too. I already didn't like her because she was fucking my girl's man.

I hung up the phone and noticed an unfamiliar number. I called it back, and it was Fatal. I was nervous to talk to her. She was a nut case and a half. I wasn't sure if I even made the right choice by calling her, but she owed Spinx a favor so what the hell.

"Umm… Fae, I need a favor, umm… I got jumped on

and I need to get those bitches back. They fucked my-"

Fae began to speak. Her voice was so tiny and high pitched. It really didn't fit her character. "Let me get this straight. You want me to come and help you fight… high school chicks? Does Braxton know you're calling me for this?" she said as if she was offended.

I know she dealt with things bigger than this, but I needed to get my point across.

"Yea, he knows." I lied. "He told me you owe him a favor."

I heard her inhale something and cough a little. "You know what? I am a little bored… you go to Wilson, right? I'll be there in a few."

I was so excited. I'd just made my first hit. It was going to be on now. Fae, aka Fatalia "Fatal" Edwards, (that was really her name) was hell's fiery in human form. You would have never known what time she was on because she was quiet and kept to herself.

She was twenty-one, about 5'6, and one hundred and forty pounds at the most. She had a caramel complexion and was a real girlie girl. At least that's what she portrayed to be. She was a straight killa', and I really mean that literally. She was from the city. She grew up around Rashawn. It was said that they were real tight when they were kids. Then something drastic happened with her mom and she went into foster care for a minute. That's when she became "Fatal."

I still wondered how she managed to do dirt for all those different people. You would think there would have been a conflict of interest at some point. I guess she didn't choose sides. It didn't matter as long as your paper was right. Spinx once told me she owed him a favor and any time I needed her to just call. I remember the first time I found out about her, one night by mistake. This fiend had beat Gizz for a lot of money and tried to snitch to 5-0. Gizz put the bug in Fae's ear, and let's just say that bitch had a closed casket.

I went upstairs to the lunch room and got a Very Fine fruit punch out the snack line. All eyes were on me. I acted like everything was cool. I sat at my usual table drinking my juice and acting like I was reading a book. Co-Co came over to me like she was concerned.

"Are you ok?" she asked, sliding into the chair next to me.

"Why wouldn't I be?" I tried to play dumb right with her.

"I mean... I saw... heard what happened, and I called Spinx. You know he's going to handle this right?" she asked.

I just looked at her. *Look at this bitch trying to convince me,* I thought. I was real cordial about her deception. "I know he will, but I'm cool though. I know if you had been there you would have helped." I took a sip of my juice eye-ing her down the whole time.

She paused. "Yeah, girl... you know if I was there we would have fucked them city bitches up." She tried to get rowdy. She held her hand out for me to give her a pound.

I rolled my eyes. *That ho must be crazy*, I thought. My pager buzzed. They were here. I left her silly ass sitting right there. I went down the back hallway by the gym and let them in. They all had on hooded sweatshirts with Tims, all black. Fae handed me the pepper spray and a concoction of bleach and ammonia in a spray bottle. A lot of girls from out the way used that to try to blind their opponents. They waited by the back steps until I did what I had to do.

I went to the upstairs lunch room and sprayed the pepper spray as I walked through. I did the entire upstairs. Within minutes people were coughing and gagging. I went to the downstairs lunch area and did the same. I met Fae at the back steps, and we waited for the announcements over the loud speaker. Everyone who was in the lunch rooms had to report to the gym and classes wouldn't be switched until the airways were cleared.

I found out from an office aide what class the chicks who banked me were in. We went straight to Small Animal Care. That's the class that bitch Drexanne was in. I targeted her because she was the first to throw a blow. It would take a long time before the administrators could get there. They had a situation to handle with the pepper spray; meaning they were going to search all those damn students to see who did it.

When we reached the classroom I looked through the glass and noticed a few other girls that jumped me were in the class, too. I pointed them out to my girls. Fae busted through the door and I sprayed one bitch with the bleach and ammonia. She screamed, holding her eyes, gasping and coughing. I started fucking her up. Muff and Buff were going to work on the other girls.

"Y'all thought y'all bitches were bad... huh. Now guess who got the last laugh!"

I threw that bitch to the floor, pinned her down and started banging her head onto the floor. Nobody was trying to break it up, not even the teacher. The girl's nose started bleeding, and I got off her and spit in her fuckin' ugly face. I motioned to the twins and they backed off the chick. That bitch wasn't moving, she was crying like a fucking baby on the floor. Fae had a grip on Drexanne's rod pony tail and flicked a razor out of her mouth. My heart started beating a mile a minute.

I screamed, "No!" but it was too late.

Fae sliced her damn face up, and blood started gushing everywhere. I wanted to throw up at the sight of the bulging white meat in her face. I ran out the room. Fae and the twins followed. We ran upstairs and some more shit was poppin' off. It was pure chaos. Bo, Lil' Don-Don, E-Skeez, and a couple of the other young boys were beating the shit out of Chauncey and his crew. Bo had a metal belt wrapped around his fist and was pounding Chauncey's face with it. He saw us and told us to bounce.

I got in the Honda wagon with Fae and the Twins. Not long afterwards the guys were behind us. I was scared, but excited at the same time. I kept looking for the cops, but none came. Thoughts of regret started to surface. I didn't want anybody to get maimed. I started to have doubts again about calling Fae. Maybe it wasn't a good idea to call her, but I wanted them bitches to know who they were fuckin' wit'. *I know they gonna try and retaliate*, I thought. My stomach starting doing flips. The picture of Fae cutting Anne's face kept replaying over in my mind. I just hoped to God I wouldn't have to reap what I sowed.

I didn't go straight home. I went down the Hill to Ms. Nett's. I had a key so I just went right in. Spade was sitting on the couch talking on the phone. He hung up.

"Yo, what the fuck happened at Wilson High today?" he laughed.

"Man, bro... you don't even want to know," I said. I stretched out across the leather love seat and kicked off my sneaks.

"You all right though... Fatal came through for you?" he asked.

"Yeah... she handled hers."

He clapped his hands. "Yeah, I know, my baby always do." He pulled out a blunt. "I'm about to spark this, you blowin' with me?"

"Yeah, I need that to relax my mind. That shit was real crazy today. I can't believe those bitches banked me."

He lit the blunt and took a pull. His mouth was full of smoke when he spoke, "Yeah, well they got what they deserved. And you know the squad beat that nigga Chauncey until he shitted himself." He laughed and exhaled.

"What?" I was laughing. "He shit himself?"

Spade said, "Yup… shit his self!"

We laughed about the earlier events and got high.

Later that afternoon I went home to check in. When I got home my mom wasn't home, but Kat was there. I walked in the door and she pushed me to the ground. I was high as hell. I tried to get up but it seemed like I was moving in slow motion. I tried to swing on her, but she caught me right in the jaw. I noticed she didn't have her regular dress-up gear on. She wore a pink and white Nike sweat suit with a pair of pink and white Air Max.

"Are fucking crazy?" she yelled. "Who cut Annie's face?"

"I DON'T KNOW WHAT THE FUCK YOU'RE TALKING ABOUT!" I screamed. I knew I was no match for Kat. She was taller and carried more weight than I did. Not to mention she could *actually* fight. I got up to my feet.

"Oh, you want to play stupid?" she said, slamming me into the wall. "You know your little friends done fucked up right? Annie is Ra-Ra's cousin; his first fucking cousin. She is in the hospital! She has over thirty-five stitches in her face. She's really fucked up!" Kat's tone was sharp.

I was holding my back in pain. I couldn't believe that she was snapping on me after what they had done to me. "I DIDN'T DO IT! DID YOU KNOW SHE BANKED ME

TODAY? YOU WORRIED ABOUT HER AND I'M YOUR FUCKIN' SISTER AND SHE BANKED ME!" I started crying.

Kat sat on the chair breathing hard. She took a deep breath and said, "I know what happened and I was going to deal with it. But you called your fake, gansta ass, cradle robbing, fuck buddy, and he sent those bitches to go beat up on high school students." She paused. "Matter of fact, where was you at during the hit?" she demanded.

I sat on the chair across from her. If my body wasn't in so much pain I would have picked up one of those wooden African figurines and busted that bitch in her head. I couldn't believe she put her hands on me.

"I don't know, you tell me since you know so much," I sobbed. "Chauncey hit me, did you know that?" I cried. My feelings were hurt. I loved my sister, but she just treated me like shit when it came to Ra-Ra and them. It was like I was her enemy since I dealt with Spinx.

She sat up in the chair and said, "Yeah, and believe me, Rashawn is making him pay for it as we speak. He looks at you like his little sister. I don't know why, you're so disloyal to him. That Spinx character has your mind all fucked up, Nalyse. He doesn't love you. If he did he would have went up there and whooped on Chauncey himself, not send his flunkies. And where is he at anyway? I heard he doesn't even live down the Hill anymore. He stays out in the Elm with his real girlfriend, Kita!"

Here she goes with this shit. She always thinks she knows something, I thought. My tears had stopped. I sucked my teeth and sarcastically said, "That's not his girlfriend. It's not like that because she told me... and he doesn't live there! He is at Ms. Nett's every night except for when he goes out of town... and I know that for a fact because I am with him every night."

Kat sighed and shook her head. She tried to sound sympathetic when she said, "You are a lost cause. Nalyse, be careful. Everything ain't always what it seems." Before she walked out the house she warned me not to go to E's party on Friday.

Chapter 4
NAUGHTY NYCE

After Kat left my brother called. Stack was in the detention center for violation of his probation. He rolled with the city boys. He said the niggas out here were whack and lived in a fairy tale world. He started putting in work for Ra-Ra shortly after we moved out here. He basically went back to the city. I guess I was the only one down for my set. We ain't live in the city no more. I can understand Kat's position, because she was with Ra-Ra since she was like thirteen, before he made it big. But my brother, Spinx tried to look out for him, but he just kept throwing him shade.

I answered the phone flatly, "Yeah... Stacks."

He didn't waste time, tearing right into me. "Yo, what's on your mine, Nyse?" he asked. "Why are you causing all this ruckus?"

Whatever happened to hey sis, how are you? I thought. "Oh, come on... you too? I ain't even trying to hear this shit. I had enough for the night... and mom is not here!" I banged on him. The phone rang again.

I grabbed my keys and walked to Ms. Netts. When I reached their street about six cars were parked in her yard. *She must be having a card game*, I thought. When I went in there were a house full of niggas. To my surprise, Brock and his boys were sitting on one side of the room. Bo, Gizz and Spinx were on the other side.

"What's up, Nyse? I heard you knockin' hoes out," said Gizz.

I smiled. "Yeah... if that's what you want to call it," I said quietly.

Spinx waved for me to come to him. All eyes were on me as I made my way through the crowded living room. He pulled me onto his lap. He pulled me close to him and asked me if I was all right. I nodded. Out the corner of my eye I could see Brock sneaking looks my way. I smiled sneakily. He was cute, and he did have the principles I lived off of, money and power. I didn't need the fuckin' respect, power overrides every thing.

Spinx moved his hand to my inner thigh and kissed me on my neck. He always did shit like this in front of his boys. I guess that was his way of proving to them that I was all his. I used to feel uncomfortable; like I was a prize possession or something, but as time went on I enjoyed putting on the little show. It just let me see who was really faithful to Spinx.

The ones that were faithful would turn their heads the other way, but I could always tell who weren't because they would have a lustful look in their eyes. Wishing they had me instead of him. Sometimes he wanted me to fuck him while they were all here, and he would ask me to scream his name and make all types of noises. I know it was to pump his ego. I didn't care. It was fun to me.

Spinx whispered to me, telling me to go upstairs and wait for him. He had to handle some business. I moved from his lap, slowly grinding my ass deep in his crouch area. Everyone was on it. He smacked my ass, and I playfully pouted. He liked that shit. I snuck another look at Brock, and we made eye contact. *Damn, he is really cute,* I thought.

I'd fallen asleep by the time Spinx got to me. I'd made sure I was ass naked. I felt him between my legs, kissing his "favorite," as he called it. I moaned.

"You up, baby?" he whispered.

"I am now." I grabbed his head and pushed him deeper into my abyss.

He continued to bite that thang until my juices was running down his chin. He sat up in the bed and admired my body. I noticed that tonight he had the red light on instead of the blue. Red usually meant we were really going to get freaky. Blue was for romance. He lay on his back and lifted my body on top of his.

I whispered in his ear as he squeezed my tits and bit down on my nipples, "Baby, do you love me?" I moaned.

In between bites he moaned, "Yes."

With that I squatted over his stiffness and slowly lowered myself down. Teasing him, I squeezed my wall muscles, causing them to grip his manhood tightly. He loved when I did that. His eyes starting rolling in the back of his head; I had him right where I wanted him. Now it was time to go in for the kill. I slid down until every inch of him filled me. My left leg began to shake. I bit my lip and held my breath. The vibrations of his pulsating muscle inside of me began to take me to another level of bliss. I tried hard to fight the wonderful feeling that was taking over, because I had to handle some business.

"Spinxy, baby… you know..." *Damn, his dick is feeling so good,* I thought. "You know… I graduate real soon and I wanted to know... wow… oh, God!"

Spinx grabbed my hips and began bouncing me up and down hard on his dick. I guess that was his way of telling me to shut the fuck up. He really was into it, because he was telling me how much he loved my pussy and I betta neva give it away. I squeezed my tits and began to enjoy the ride. He was cupping my ass cheeks, lifting his pelvis, causing our bodies to meet and smack against each other. I was really working my shit.

"Damn, baby, you must have really missed me," he said.

That made me snap back. For a minute there I was imagining he was Brock. *I'm fuckin' up*, I thought. When I thought he was about to cum I tightened my walls.

"Damn," he said. "This shit feels so good."

I went in for the kill. "Baby, what are you getting me for my graduation?" I asked.

He responded, "Oohh, you can get... ohh... ssssss… whateva you want."

I was working him. "I want a car... a nice car, a cell phone, take me to my prom and I want you to send me to college."

"Aight, whateva you want. Just keep giving me that juicy, phat pussy," he begged.

I gave it to him gladly. I put his black ass straight to sleep.

I woke up and it was 6 am. *Oh shit!* I thought. I had to get home before my mom did. She was working from 11 pm until 7 am. I grabbed my clothes and threw them on. The brightness from the sun was blinding me as I sprinted up the hill and through the path to get to my house. I sighed in relief when I didn't see my mom's car in the driveway. I showered and got ready for school.

When my mom came home she looked tired.

I gave her a kiss on the cheek. "You all right, mommy?" I asked. I erased the message on the answer machine from Mr. Scott. He'd called to tell my mother I was suspended for fighting. She already had too much on her mind to deal with that petty shit.

"Yeah, baby, just tired," she replied.

I noticed she didn't close the door behind her. I went to go shut it.

"Lyse, you can leave that open. I'm getting some clothes. I'm going to stay the weekend with Mr. Dave. You want to go to your sister's or will you be all right here?" she asked, kissing me on the cheek.

"Oh, I'll be all right. I'm gonna stay here. There's a party tonight that I wanted to go to... if it's cool with you?" I snuck in.

"Go ahead. Just be careful. You know how wild those guys are out here." She went in her purse and handed me a couple of dollars and went upstairs to pack.

When she was out of sight I started jumping up and down. I was hyped. I could be with my baby all weekend. I sat on the couch and waited for her to leave. We gave each other a kiss and she was out the door. I didn't tell her about the fight and how I was suspended for the day. She would never know anyway, unless Kat told her. She didn't even know about Spinx. In her eyes I was still sweet and virtuous Lyse.

I grabbed my backpack and went to the bus stop just in case she forgot something. When the bus pulled up I got on and rode until he hit the bus stop near Ms. Netts. I told the bus driver that I forgot to lock my door and he let me off. I waited until he pulled off and walked across the street.

The door was already unlocked. Spade was on his way out the door. He looked cute, as always. He had on a pair of Levi's and a cute button up Ralph Lauren. He told me Doris was cooking breakfast. He had a plate in his hand, it looked good, too. I was starving. When I went to the dining room Ms. Nett was sitting at the table eating. She had on a leopard nightie, with a bonnet over her head. *She must have had company last night*, I thought. To be a big woman Ms. Nett kept a fine nigga with money in her presence.

"Hey, baby," she said, extending her arms for me to give her a hug. "Why ain't you in school?"

She pulled a Newport out of the pack and lit it.

I start singing that *Kris Kross* song and danced around, "I missed the bus.... I missed the bus."

She busted out laughing. "Girl you are retarded!"

I smiled and grabbed a plate. "Thanks, Ms. Doris."

She smiled. I felt bad for her. She was really sweet, but she was on that crack bad. She was like their housekeeper. She cooked, cleaned and did the laundry for some rock. Spinx justified it by saying at least he wasn't taking her SSI check. I hated the way people talked to her. I wanted to snap for her sometime. I sat next to Ms. Nett and dug into my food like I ain't never ate in my life. It was so quiet alls you could hear was me smacking and my fork hitting the plate. I looked up and they were staring at me.

"What! Why are y'all staring at me?" I said with a mouth full.

"Damn… bitch, breathe! If I didn't know any better I would have thought you ain't eat in months!"

Ms. Nett took another pull of her cigarette while she watched me devour my food.

I chewed my food and swallowed. "I'm hungry! Ms. Nett, I'm always hungry," I said, picking up more food to put in my mouth.

She placed the Newport in the ashtray and studied my face. "Nyse, when the last time you been on?" inquired Ms. Nett.

"Yesterday when I came home from school," I said. Assuming, but not really knowing what she was talking about.

"Yuck… and you Braxton were fucking last night like dogs in heat! I hope you washed them bloody ass sheets!" she said with a repugnant expression on her face.

I was confused. "Ms. Nett, what are you talking about, darling?" I asked.

"Don't darling me... bitch! I'm talking about your nasty ass fucking on your period!"

She pulled out another Newport and rolled her eyes.

"I'm not on my period." I laughed. "I thought you were talking about the last time I smoked gank!"

She took a deep pull of the Newport and laughed as smoked seeped from her nostrils. "You's a silly bitch! I ain't talking bout no damn weed. You pregnant, Nyse? Your face getting a little full and he sleeps all the fucking time. You ready to make me a grandma *again* at thirty-eight?" she asked before she put the cancer stick to her lips.

I snickered. "Yeah, right! I'm hardly knocked." I grabbed my plate and put it in the sink.

"Where you goin'?" Ms. Nett asked.

"To bed!" I shouted and skipped towards the steps.

She snorted. "Yeah, with your legs up!"

I heard her and Ms. Doris bust out laughing. But she wasn't lying. I was gonna hop on the dick again. Morning dick was the best.

Later that afternoon, I called the twins to find out what they were wearing to the party. They said they still didn't know. I called Kee to see how she was. Her little sister answered the phone and told me she was at her aunt's in Chester.

Around 9:00 pm everybody was getting dressed to go to E-Skeez's party. The guys were downstairs making arrangements in case something popped off. Brock and his Eastside boys were going to be there too, but they were neutral. Brock supplied Spinx when he couldn't get weight from his connect. He was also affiliated with Ra-Ra, so he was like the middleman sometimes. I always thought Spinx was a nut for dealing with the same people Rashawn did. He didn't see it as a threat. I got tired of arguing with him about it. I just had a deep feeling it was going to one day bite him in the ass. He'd really put trust in Brock. He was E's cousin so he thought that made a big difference. It didn't convince me none.

I was in Spinx's room getting dressed for the party. I decided to wear a pair of black DKNY jeans and a black and silver signature DKNY shirt. I wrapped my hair so it lay flat on my shoulders. I threw on a pair of black field Tims, just in case things did get a little out of hand. Everyone was on high alert because I told Spinx how my sister didn't want me to go to E's party. I guess he took heed to the warning. I went downstairs, smoke was everywhere as usual. Someone passed me the blunt. I looked at Spinx for approval. He nodded and I hit it.

Twenty minutes later the twins and Caree came to get me. They all looked nice. The twins had on jeans and Hilfiger T-shirts. Caree, on the other hand, had on some shit Kat would wear only it wasn't name brand. You could tell by the material she got that shit from Dots, but it was still cute. She had on a black cat suit, with this silver chain belt that hugged every curve on her body and black rider boots with a fat heel. Her auburn hair, that matched perfect with her cinnamon skin, was in Janet Jackson braids. You know; the ones she wore in Poetic Justice.

Caree went to our school and hung out sometimes. I didn't like her at first, because I would catch Spinx looking at her all the time. When I found out she wasn't interested we became cool. She had a college boyfriend who didn't want her really hanging out with "hood people." She was quiet, but fun to be around when she was feeling it.

It was a nice evening so we decided to walk up the Hill to E's house. We were laughing and joking about the fight. When we got to the party it was jumpin'. It was so crowded you could barely walk through. The DJ was playing *T.A.* (Top Authority) *"Never Leave Home Without It."* Everybody was hyped. Stankin' ass Meekie's ass was trying to dance. She had a bottle of Henny in her hand, grindin' on some young boy.

We made our way to the back of the room. Caree pulled out a bottle of Seagram's Gin and two forty once bottles of Crazy Horse. We poured the gin in the bottles and drank them. The twins didn't drink, they just smoked. After about twenty minutes I was feeling it, sweating and shit. That's when I noticed everyone had dipped off. I was cool with it.

My song came on by *Sasha, "Kill the Bitch.*" I started doing the butterfly. I broke it down to the floor. I started to tick and gyrate my body like I was straight from the Motherland. I had those niggas drooling. Meekie even stopped shakin' her old ass to watch my performance. That's when I spotted Brock standing against the wall. I was so drunk that I decided to fuck with him like I did Dale.

I moved towards him dancing. I bent over and bounced my ass against his manhood. I was so fucked up I didn't even care who saw what I was doing. I looked him in the eyes while I enticed him. He tried to keep a straight face, but I felt his shit getting hard as cement. I guess the DJ was enjoying the show, because he played *Mad Cobra's "Flex."* I really threw it on Brock. He placed his hands around my hips as I slow whined him.

I wrapped my arms around his neck and whispered, "Do you want to fuck me?"

He licked his lips and whispered in my ear, "Stop playing

games with that knuckle head man of yours and I'll show what it's like to be with a real nigga." He gently moved me from in front of him and got lost in the crowd.

Hmm... sounds good, I thought. But I wasn't about to let Spinx go. *Not yet*. I had to see if he was going to come through for my graduation. If he reneged then I might take him up on his offer. *I just might do that,* I thought. *He wants me*. I took a swig of my concoction and went back for another bottle. I felt a little queasy so I detoured to the bathroom. I opened the door and found Muff on her knees with E-Skeez's balls smacking up against her chin.

I shut the door and yelled, "That's what bedrooms are for!"

I went upstairs to try the other one. I opened the door and this one was cool. I got on my knees and knelt in front of the toilet seat. I gagged, but nothing came out. I did need to piss though. I pissed for what seemed like fifteen minutes. I thought I was never going to stop. I washed my hands and went back to the party. It seemed like fifty more people came.

I saw Spade standing up against the wall talking shit to some young girl. I went over to them. Soon as he saw me he dismissed her. She was pissed. She rolled her eyes and slipped him her number before she disappeared. We laughed and clowned a few people who thought they were fly but truly looked a mess.

Spade and I danced through a few songs. I was having a ball. The DJ turned on "*Throw Ya Gunz*" by *Onyx,* and mutha fuckas got out of control. He threw the strobe light on and everybody was partying, jumping all around and rhyming with Sticky Fingaz. "What's mine is mine and what yours is mine..." That's my shit! We were so into it, no one paid attention to the fact Chauncey and his boys came in waving a .22.

Dawg, who was from the Hills, was in the corner the

whole time scoping everything out. He shouted, "I'M ABOUT TO LET LOOSE!"

Everyone turned around as he pulled a sawed-off shot gun out his trench coat. Everyone started to run immediately. It was so crowded that everyone was stepping over each other trying to get out. The DJ was even going to leave his shit behind. I was scared to death. I started to run out the back door; then I remembered my girls. I couldn't leave them behind.

I felt someone trying to pull me out the house. When we got outside there was unknown cars everywhere. I looked at the hand that was pulling me and it was Muff. We saw Caree and Buff hiding behind the car. I was so relieved to see them. We ran through the path to get to the set. Buff got clothes lined (literally) by someone's clothes line. She was on the ground grabbing her throat. I helped her up.

We heard a big boom coming from E's house. I started screaming. We were all crying. We got to the big field and I paused. It was so dark that you couldn't see anything but the tall weeds. I was a little hesitant to go through them, but that was the quickest way I could get to my house. I thought, *these niggas is from the city, they don't know nothin' about our paths.* I figured this would be the safest route. We were about to make a run for it, but I stopped when I saw someone standing in the dark by a tree. I moved in a little closer and noticed it was Reap, aka The Reaper.

He yelled, "Nyse, get the fuck on the ground."

We all dropped in a synchronized fashion to the ground. We heard gunfire over our heads. I lay in the grass shaking hysterically. Caree was crying and pissed herself. I heard something down on the ground coming our way. I looked around and noticed it was Skeez.

He said in a hushed tone, "Y'all need to get the fuck outta

here. When we say run, run your ass home!" Skeez was on his damn stomach like army commando.

Everything got silent and out of no where Reap yelled, "Run!"

We all ran. I ran on the set and under the light pole. I saw an all too familiar souped-up gold Acura Legend. *Damn*, I thought. It was Ra-Ra. His guard was standing outside the car. He had on a Carhartt camouflage outfit and combat boots. He was ready to go to war. I tried to run away from him.

"Nalyse!" he yelled.

I tried to ignore him, but I couldn't. Rashawn had never done anything to me, and I doubted if he would do anything to hurt me. I stopped and faced his direction. I was stuck between a rock and a hard place. Spinx was my man, but Rashawn was like family. He always looked out for me. I started walking towards him. I heard my girls screaming for me to run, but I couldn't. He started to walk towards me. I was feeling confused, scared and anxious.

Rashawn didn't look like he could hurt a fly. He was brown skin with a baby face and deep dimples; standing 6'0 with bow legs. He reminded me so much of that boxer "Sugar" Shane Mosley, eyes and all. You would've never known he was a trigga-happy, hot head when provoked. He was so calm and cool you wouldn't have even known he was in the middle of a flat out war.

I became mesmerized by his conduct. We were standing face to face. My heart raced, not out of fear; to my surprise it was from pure lust. I had to check myself. For some reason I was being turned on; I had to shake this feeling. *It has to be the weed and alcohol, or my adrenaline is too high*, I thought. I had never paid attention to how attractive he was in the past. I tried to avoid eye contact. I didn't want him to be able to read my thoughts, because they were written all over my face. His hand gently caressed my face. He was being sweet, yet showed authority.

"I'm not mad at you, lil' sis, but you need to get your ass home. Because shit about to be hectic… we'll talk about this soon, ok?"

He gave me a quick hug and pushed me along.

I was feeling tingling sensations in places I had no business feeling them. I took one more look at him before I ran towards my house. I was only a few houses away from my destination, before I was cut off by an unpleasant but familiar face. Chauncey was standing in front of me grinning. I looked behind me for help but Ra-Ra was long gone. He grabbed me by my arm. I began screaming immediately. I noticed his face was slightly disfigured. He pushed me to the ground and pointed at his face.

He grinded his teeth when he said, "Bitch... this is your fault." He pulled a gun from the back of his pants and stuck it to my head.

I screamed for help, hoping one of the neighbors would call the cops. But I knew that was a lost cause. Those people loved to see drama. He began to unzip his pants. *I know this nigga ain't about to rape me,* I thought. I would never know what his plans were. I heard several popping noises. Next, I watched his body hit ground with blood spilling from his mouth. I let out another scream. I couldn't move. I had never seen anyone shot right in front of me. Brock walked over to me with the barrel of his gun smoking. I was shaking out of control. He pulled me from the ground.

"You ok?"

I didn't answer. I heard police sirens in the distance.

"Run, Nyse! Go the fuck home," he ordered.

I snapped out of it and ran as fast as I could. I got in front of my house, but stopped at my curb. I was too scared to go in. It was so dark and my mom didn't leave the outside light on. I heard movement behind the bushes. I was ready to break out until I saw Caree come from behind them followed by the twins. Caree hugged me and cried. They thought something happened to me. I gave her the keys and we went in the house.

Once inside, I told them that Chauncey tried to rape me and he was now dead. Everyone was hysterical. It seemed like out of nowhere lights started to flash outside. You could hear the helicopters flying over the house and see spotlights from them lighting up the paths. They were in the paths with dogs. I left the girls in the window. I went to my room and cried. I had no doubt in my mind that this was my fault. The question in my mind was if I was gonna have to answer for it.

Chapter 5
MIXED EMOTIONS

I sat up all night with the phone next to me. The twins and Caree were knocked out on the couches. I kept calling Kat, but she didn't answer. I lay in my bed playing out the night's events. So much was happening and I was feeling so many different emotions. I tried to figure out the feeling that came over me when Ra and I were face to face. I don't know if it was the excitement or what. I know I never felt that way in his presence before. I blamed it on the alcohol. Then there was Brock, I was basically begging him to fuck me. I just hoped that everyone forgot about my little show and it didn't get back to Spinx.

I went over to the window and glanced out. It was still hot outside. It was just starting to get light. There were cops everywhere. I paged Spinx several times last night, but no call back. Everything just kept playing back in my mind. Then I thought about Brock. *Oh my God, he saved my life*, I thought. I prayed that he was not locked up for laying down Chauncey.

Around 7 am my phone rang, I answered it on the first ring. "Hello," I whispered.

"Didn't I tell your ass to stay home? Who's in the house with you?"

You could hear it all in Kat's voice that she was vexed.

"Caree and the twins," I said timidly.

"Meet me at the back door!" she demanded, and hung up.

I did as I was told. I went downstairs to the kitchen to open the back door. She was standing out back by the fence wearing a black hoody and a pair of Gap sweat pants. I walked over to her.

"Why are you out here?" I asked.

"Look, I can't stay long. You need to stay away from Ms. Nett's, it's real hot. Chauncey got sprayed and he's dead. A few others got hit and many a few got locked up. Rashawn is livid. I can't be out here for a while... until things die down. I will call you and let you know... what I can. But you need to leave that nigga alone like yesterday," she said.

I started to cry. "What if I can't?" I said. "What if I can't because I'm pregnant?"

Disappointment was all over her face. She was blasé when she said, "Lyse, that's why there's a thing called abortion... I will gladly pay for it. I love you, sis. Just do me a favor, and stay the fuck away from that MAN!"

We exchanged quick hugs, and she disappeared into the woods. I went back in the house. I was getting a bottle of coke from the fridge when I heard movement in the living room. I went to investigate. Muff was just waking up, her eyes were all puffy. I gave her a hug.

"You all right?" I asked.

"Yeah," she replied.

I told her she could stay as long as she wanted. We sat there in silence waiting to hear from people. I heard a knock at my door. I peeked through the blinds, and it was Spinx, Gizz and two other guys. I opened it up and hugged Spinx real tight. He pulled me into the kitchen. He seemed angry.

"Did you tell your sister's people where I be at?" he said,

heated.

"Huh… I don't-,"

He cut me off and pushed me into the wall. He was annoyed and yelled, "Don't fucking play with me, Nyse. Those mutha fuckas pointed a gun at my mom's head, stole my pack and shot a few of my young boys. Who were you talking around?"

I started crying out of control. "I don't know! I didn't tell anyone. I don't talk about your business or where you live! No one knows!" I cried.

I thought about the conversation I had with my sister the other day. Damn! I shook my head. I told her about him being at Ms. Nett's.

"You remembering something, Nyse... what's all the expressions about?" he spat.

I had to think fast. There was no way I was gonna tell him that my sister did it. Then it came to me.

I calmly said, "Yeah, Co-Co, the day of the fight. She talked about how you was gonna handle shit and something about the niggas at Ms. Netts. We were in the cafeteria and you know our school is flooded with those Westside people." I lied.

Caree heard what was going on. She came in and co-signed my lie. She said she was in the snack line and heard her. Spinx looked at Caree, then me. He gave me a hug and apologized. He told me that he had to get missing for a minute. None of his immediate crew would be around for a minute, but Brock would look after me for him. I asked about Ms. Nett and he told me to go check on her later. Before he left out I told him I think I might be pregnant. He said his mom already told him and we would talk about it when he called me.

After they left I pulled Caree in the bathroom. "Why you

lie for me?" I asked.

"Because you're my peoples and I know what he does to bitches he thinks betrayed him," she said.

I was puzzled.

"It's *Fatal*," she said, and walked out.

I received a phone call later that evening from Brock. I answered and was happy to hear his voice. "Thank you so much for saving my life," I said. I was feeling like a school girl talking to her first boy on the phone.

He laughed. "Wow... I didn't know a phone call could do so much," he joked. "But I know what you mean, and I'd rather discuss that face to face," he said.

He started speaking in code then I caught on. The damn phones might be tapped. He told me he would come check me out late night.

•••••••••••••••••••••••••••••••

I couldn't believe what went down. I hadn't heard from Spinx since the night he left. He'd promised to call me once he got to wherever he was going. But of course he didn't. I thought about what Caree said. I doubted very much if he would ever sick Fae on me. He loved me way too much. That nigga cried many nights, telling me he couldn't live without me, he couldn't hurt me. I spoke to Ms. Nett and she was regular. It seemed as if it didn't even affect her that a gun was put to her head and her house was ransacked. She still had her weekly card game in spite of it.

Brock stopped by the night after everything went down. He didn't do much talking. I told him that the cops were going door to door asking questions. He told me not to worry about it and said that nothing would come back on me. We smoked a blunt and watched *Faces of Death*. I cuddled next to him during the scary parts, and he put his arm around me. He didn't try anything, he was a perfect gentlemen.

We fell asleep on my couch. We both slept long and hard. We didn't get up until 2 pm the next day. He told me he had to make a few runs and he bounced. He was real cool peoples. Most niggas would have tried to get some, especially after what I said to him at the party. God knows I would have wanted to give it to him if he'd tried. But I couldn't, especially since I wasn't sure if I was carrying Spinx's baby.

••••••••••••••••••••••••••••••

It was Monday morning and I was at the bus stop waiting for my bus. Everyone was giving me ice grills. I knew they blamed me for all the chaos that went down, but I didn't give a fuck. What could they do to me? I stared straight ahead, not even wanting to give them the satisfaction of looking their way.

I heard one chick that spoke with a horrible lisp say, "You hear what happened to Co-Co?"

Her little friend with the raggedy ass Bakka braids was like, "Yeah, that nigga Bo beat the shit out of her, something about she set his boy up."

I was in shock. I couldn't believe he had something done to her.

The lispy chick said, "That shit pissed me off, because the person who should have their ass beat is sitting pretty... HER ass should be sitting in Christiana Hospital, not Co-Co," she stressed her words.

I couldn't help myself. I looked back at them and smiled.

The lisp chick acted as if she wanted to jump. I shook me finger and calmly said, "Now, darling, you know that's a no... no. I know you don't want to end up like your friend." I gave her a wicked smile as the bus pulled up.

She looked steamed.

I sat in the front seat just in case some shit popped off. I really wasn't in the mood for that. On the ride to school I heard them talking cash shit in the back. I thought to myself, *they just showing off because Spinx ain't around.* I couldn't wait until he came back. I was going to tell him about all the skeez bitches and the gay ass niggas gossiping with them.

I went straight to the Wellness Center when we arrived at school. I saw a bunch of people gathering in the hallway discussing the events that happened at the party. Some were even crying. I hurried pass them all before anyone could get enough courage to say anything to me. When I entered the office the secretary even had a look on her face like she felt some type of way. I rolled my eyes and kept it moving. They were just pissed because Chauncey was their star basketball player. *Oh well… nigga should have kept his hands to himself,* I thought. I signed my name on the clipboard and waited for the nurse. Five minutes later Mrs. Long came strolling in.

"Nalyse, why are you here so early in the morning. Have you even been to home room?" she asked.

"I have a problem," I whimpered. I threw on some fake tears. "I think I may be pregnant and I didn't know who else to turn too."

"Ohh, Nalyse, sweetie… oh my… you're about to graduate, right?" her face wrinkled with concern.

I nodded.

"Look," she said, handing me a specimen cup and 2 wipes. She spoke to me in a voice that you would use with a preschooler, "Go to the bathroom wipe yourself clean, you know the proper way to wipe... correct? I want you to pee-pee in this cup and bring it back to me."

I wanted to laugh, but I had to play the distressed role. I went to the bathroom and handled my business. I sat the cup of urine on the counter. She told me she would call me down after homeroom was over to give me the results and counsel me. I told her ok. I didn't want any damn counseling. I just needed the results.

I went to the cafeteria to grab some donuts. Duncan Donuts came to our school in the morning. I was dying for some glazed and cream filled. I walked passed a crowd of city people who were staring me down. No one said a word, they just looked. I stood in line waiting my turn. I was getting impatient. I was starting to feel sick and I needed something in my stomach quick. The line didn't seem to be moving. I said "fuck it," and sulked.

I went over to the soda machine to get a ginger ale. I was putting my money in the machine when I noticed I was being surrounded. I looked to my left and it was Ms. Lipsy and the Bakka Braid Beast. I continued getting my shit. They were from my set, and I knew they weren't going to do anything.

I heard someone on my right say, "Stay the fuck from down my man's house... he don't want your stank ass no more."

I laughed as I turned to see who let such foolishness run from their lips. Whoever this bitch was, she was tripping. I looked up and it was Shay, Meekie's fifteen year old daughter. I laughed even more. She looked stank as always. She had on a pair of painted-on, acid wash jeans and this old ass Nautica T-shirt.

I said, "You busted bitch, he wouldn't touch your yok ass with a dead nigga's dick." I proceeded to walk away.

That's when I heard someone get on the table and yell, "LET'S GET READY TO RUMBLE!" Shay grabbed me by my ponytail, pulling me back and started swinging. It was on. I managed to keep my leverage and started fighting back. I got a good hold on her and started slamming her into lunch tables, knocking them over. I was so mad, not because she hit me, but I was fucking hungry and it was too early for this bullshit. I heard some nigga crying like a bitch... "MAKE THEM STOP, WE ARE NOT SUPPOSED TO FIGHTING ONE ANOTHER, STOP THE QUEENS FROM FIGHTING!"

Someone pulled her back first, and I got a real good hit. I tagged that bitch straight in her eye. I tried to knock it straight out of her head. Mr. Scott grabbed both of us by the arms and dragged us to the office. He took Shay to the nurse's office and directed me to his. I sat down and he closed the door behind us. He stood there for a minute. There was a knock at the door and it was Mrs. Long, the nurse. She gave Mr. Scott a look, and he sat down at his seat.

She came over to me and said, "Uh..., Nalyse... you need to go to the hospital to get checked out. I know you were just in a fight last week and now today. This is not good for the baby." She was a little uneasy when delivering the news.

I was astounded. "Baby… I'm pregnant?" I sat straight up in my seat.

"Yes, sweetie, you are… and I think it will be best if you did not return after your suspension. I am placing you on home school. It will only be for a few weeks. Graduation is the first of June anyway." She hugged me. "Do you want me to call your mother to pick you up?" she asked, sounding really concerned.

I told her I was cool and could get my own ride home. After Mrs. Long left, Mr. Scott picked up the phone.

"Yo... what are you doing?" I asked defensively.

"I'm calling your mother, Nalyse. She needs to know what just happened," he said.

"She's out of town." I lied. "Call my sister Katina, she's in charge," I said with desperation.

He paused. "Very well, what's her number?" he asked.

I gave it to him. He explained to her about the fight and said he also needed to talk to her about something concerning my health. He hung up and told me she would be there in ten minutes.

Kat and I were driving back to her place. She couldn't be seen out my way yet, Ra-Ra had told her he wanted things to calm down a bit. I told her I would have found a way home, but she wasn't having it. She didn't think I was safe there either, being as though it was a chick from my neighborhood that I had the fight with. We rode in silence. I was grateful, because I was not trying to hear shit she had to say.

I had enough on my mind, *Pregnant, ain't this a bitch?* Then that bitch Shay wanted to claim to be fucking my man. I knew that was a lie. I was at Ms. Nett's damn near everyday, even when he wasn't there. I knew she wasn't over there. Her mom probably put her up to saying that. She was probably still mad because she wasn't in the SL500. Speaking of the SL500, I wondered what happened to it. I hadn't seen him drive it in a while.

We pulled up into her driveway. She pushed the button on her visor to open the garage. I had to admit. She had it going on. He'd bought her a luxury car, three bedroom single family home, and a college education. All this at the age of twenty; most people my mother's age didn't live the way Kat did. We went into the house. I headed to the fridge to make something to eat because I was starving. Kat stood at the counter watching me. I ignored her and pulled out the eggs and bacon.

"After you eat I'm taking you to Christiana Hospital. We need to see how far you are," she said, sitting her black leather Coach bag on the granite counter top.

I continued cooking, ignoring her comment. "You want some breakfast?" I asked.

She pulled out a stool and sat down. "No, thank you… if you're less than three months you can still get an abortion here. If you are over, we're going to have to go to New York to get it done." She pulled out a phone book from under the cabinet and starting thumbing through the yellow pages.

I couldn't help but to think, *she has a lot of damn nerve trying to tell me what I'm about to do*. I put my bacon in the microwave and set the timer. I faced my sister.

I calmly, yet sarcastically stated, "What makes you think that I'm going to kill my baby? I know it comes naturally to you, being as though you have killed like four of them, but that's not how I'm going to handle this. I'm having my child... Spinx want our baby." I was annoyed at this point.

I knew I struck a nerve. Kat was like the abortion queen, she'd had so many that she couldn't get anymore in her name. Ra-Ra started paying others to use their identity so she could get them. She slammed the phonebook shut, stood up and pointed her finger in my face.

"You know what? You are a silly little bitch!"

I backed up because I thought this was going to be a continuation from the ass kicking she gave me when Annie got sliced.

"This is not about me. I made the right decisions. *Rashawn* was by my side. I didn't get rid of those babies because he didn't want them. *I* didn't want them. What I look like having a baby by his ass when he was out there sticking up people and hustling on the corners? What if he got locked up, or even killed. Then I would have had a fatherless child.

I would've ended up just like mommy, working doubles and not being there for my fucking kids!

That's why we are so messed up now. Stack is in jail; you are just lost, fucking a grown-ass man and starting shit! Starving for attention; I was so money hungry, I started messing with a murderous drug dealer just so I could have nice things, because mommy couldn't do it!" she shouted, tears welded up in her eyes.

I never saw her so upset. I stood there watching her performance. I was interrupted by the beeping sound of the microwave. I sighed, my eggs needed to be tended too. Kat was crying, but I couldn't feel anything for her. *Oh well,* I thought. It was all a show so I could agree to the abortion. I turned away and finished making my breakfast. I heard her running up the stairs. *She thinks I'm stupid. I'm not falling for that shit,* I thought. I'm having my damn baby. I took a bite of my eggs and I was in heaven. I was happy that I finally was eating.

Later that afternoon my pager went off. I checked it and saw that it was Spinx's cell. I grabbed the phone, but had second thoughts. Damn... I can't call him from my sister's. He would snap if he knew I was here. I decided to walk across the road to the Acme Market. I would use their pay phone to call.

I went to Kat's room to tell her where I was headed. When I got to her door I heard soft moans. Her door was cracked and her legs were wrapped around some dude's neck. I cracked the door a little wider to get a closer look. *Who the fuck is that?* I wondered. It damn sure wasn't Ra-Ra. Dude had his face buried in her pussy. I watched the show for a few minutes hoping I could catch a glimpse of his face. He seemed as if he had gotten lost in her jungle. He wasn't finding his way out any time soon, so I decided to leave.

That sneaky bitch. After all that shit Ra-Ra has done for her she is fucking someone else. Loyalty, that bitch bumped her head. She had the nerve to say I wasn't loyal, I thought. Obviously she didn't know the definition. I picked up the pay phone and dialed Spinx's number. It rang forever. *I guess he's not picking up because he doesn't recognize the number,* I thought. I hung up. The phone rang back like twenty seconds later. I looked around, and then answered it.

A woman's voice asked, "Hello... did someone just call my cell phone?"

I was instantly vexed. "Who the fuck is this? I called my man's cell... why the fuck are you calling me back on it?"

The voice said, "Nyse"?

"Yeah, who the fuck is you?" I asked.

"Girl, this is Kita... hold on, Spinx is right here." She laughed.

I wondered why she was with him while he was hiding out. I was getting frustrated and I needed questions answered.

"What's up, babe?" he said. "I heard what went down at school... you all right?"

I wasn't trying to hear that shit, I wanted answers. "Spinx, are you fucking little Shay? And why is Kita with you?" I demanded.

"Come on now, Nyse. I'm calling to check on you and you already know I'm under stress and you gonna start bombarding me with these silly questions. How's my baby? Is everything all right?" he said, ignoring my question.

"Are you fucking Shay?" I demanded. I wasn't letting him change the subject.

"No, I'm not fucking her. She gave me a few private strip shows and sucked on my meat. But no, I'm not fucking Shay," he said calmly.

My heart was beating a mile a minute. I didn't want to hear that shit. "So you got mom and daughter sucking on your dick. That's some nasty shit. What about Kita, you fucking her?" I asked. I wasn't prepared for what he was getting ready to say.

"Yeah, she gives me ass from time to time. It's nothing serious. She knows *you* my baby. We used to fuck around when I was at Del State, but we just friends now. That shouldn't bother you because you are my main girl. *I love you* and *they* know that," he said in arrogance.

I was livid. I was feeling light headed. My hands began to shake uncontrollably. I didn't know what to say. "I want an abortion!" I said with a shaky voice. I refused to cry.

"Woo. Hold up! What you say? I know you ain't say you was killing my seed?" said Spinx. His cockiness quickly disappeared.

"Yes, that's exactly what I said. Let one of your skeez bitches have your baby because I'm not!" I said, hurt.

I slammed the phone down and ran away from it. I heard it ringing, but I ignored it. My pager started to go off. I took it and threw it in the street. I ran all the way back to my sister's house. I ran inside and threw myself on the couch and cried. I was so stupid. *How could he do this to me?* I thought.

Chapter 6
FAMILY AFFAIR

I woke up to a bunch of commotion. My sister was laughing as loud as she could. She was talking on the phone to one of her Sorors. I slowly sat up on the couch. My head was pounding and my body was aching. I checked my watch and it was 11 pm. *Damn, this day is still not over,* I thought. It seemed to be the longest and worst day of my life. I got up to go to the bathroom. I had to pee really badly.

I was washing my hands and looked at the mirror. My eyes were puffy and red. I had three long scratches on my neck. It looked like Krueger got me in my sleep. "Stinkin' bitch," I said out loud. "I can't believe that she was fucking him." I knew Spinx said it was just a lil' head action and live entertainment, but I didn't believe that. Spinx loved to fuck and I was sure she gave it up. Meekie should be ashamed of herself, allowing her daughter to fuck a man that she was sucking off. What type of twisted shit was that?

I looked at my face and body. I looked better than that bitch. She wasn't even cute. She was bald head and had no dress game. The only thing she had going for her was her body. Like her mother she was a brick house. I mean, I had it together, too, but Shay was thick to be fifteen. That was bothering me, too. Spinx wouldn't touch me until I turned sixteen.

Then the Kita situation… he had been fucking her the whole time, before he even started messing with me. They lived together, which meant that he was getting it on a regular basis. And now he took her with him; I wondered where they were. The thoughts were beginning to overwhelm me. I cried real good, I had to get it out. I kicked the trash can, knocked shit over. I just needed to let it all out. After fifteen minutes of wrecking the bathroom, I left. Kat was standing at the door with her arms folded.

"I know... I know you were right," I snapped.

Kat tried to hug me, but I pulled away. I went to the den and sat on the camel colored leather recliner.

She followed behind me. "Sis, I tried to tell you about him... but you wouldn't listen. So what made you finally come to your senses?" she asked.

"I asked him about Shay and Kita and he told me the truth... that he was fucking them. The sad thing is, he was real chill about it," I said. I looked to see her expression when I told her he was messing with Shay, but for some reason she didn't seem surprised.

"Well, you don't need him anyway," she said. "You're about to graduate in four weeks, and after this summer you can leave to go away to school."

"I can't leave and go away, Kat, I'm pregnant. I'm not getting rid of my baby," I said.

She rolled her eyes and was about to start going off on me so I hurried and added, "So, is Rashawn coming back tonight? I saw him earlier and you guys seemed a little busy, so I didn't interrupt," I said sarcastically.

Her jaw dropped.

I smiled. She was caught up and for once in her life

speechless. "Did you hear what I said, Kat? Is Ra-Ra coming back tonight?" I politely asked.

She stood up and paced around the room. "Nalyse..., I umm... let me explain something to you."

I cut her off. "Oh there's nothing to explain... I clearly saw that you had some other nigga's face all up in your pussy. How can you do that to Ra-Ra after all he has done for you?" I shouted. For some reason I was pissed about her doing Rashawn wrong.

She became enraged. "After all he's done for me? You're right; he has done a lot of materialistic things for me. What he didn't do was be there for me physically and emotionally. He's always away doing business. I can't marry him like we planned, because he has all these enemies that will hurt me when they can't get to him. I can't visit my own mom, because I'm a target. We can't even live together. I go to his condo or we go on trips to spend real time with each other. I can't even have a real relationship with you because we are on opposite sides. That's not a real relationship. I want to be married with children someday, not always looking behind my back, being secretive about everything. That's not what I want!"

She picked up a figurine and threw it against the wall. She was on some distressed white girl shit.

"I don't like going to bed alone... so yes, I have a friend. I met him at school last year. He knows I have a man, he doesn't know anything about him. He just knows that he is powerful, has money and is not to be fucked with," she explained.

I was confused. "So, what if Ra-Ra comes here and he is here?" I asked.

"Ra-Ra doesn't come here at all. I picked the house out and he gave me the money. He has only seen pictures of this house. He's afraid the Feds or one of his enemies may follow him here."

For some reason I found that hard to believe. Why would he pay for something he didn't have access too. I didn't believe her little story; it had to be more to it. I didn't feel bad for her, she's ungrateful. She knew what she was getting into. She's a fuckin' hypocrite. She acted as if she had her shit together. She was just as fucked up as I was, if not worst. I knew she had to be lonely in this big ass house. Well, I guess not if she had dude over here banging her on the regular.

"Well if you don't mind... I want to stay here with you until I have the baby. You know, so mom won't have to worry about me," I said. I just wanted to see what really was going on over here. *Who knows, maybe her disloyalty may work in my favor*, I thought.

She hurried over to me and hugged me. I guessed that was a yes.

••••••••••••••••••••••••••••••••

It was the Memorial Day weekend. Caree came over to spend it with me. My sister and Ra-Ra went to Myrtle Beach for Black Bike Week. I opted to stay behind. Brock and his boy Roc were coming over. We were going to watch movies and order out. Brock, or should I say Kevin, and I had become close over the last few weeks. He didn't like me calling him by his street name. He would rather I call him Kevin.

The day after my break down, I called my mom to tell her I wanted to stay with Kat. She was a little upset at first, but I told her it wasn't anything she had done. I just needed to get away from that area. She said she understood. I didn't tell her I was pregnant, she would have lost it. I was just gonna wait until after graduation. Before we hung up she told me some guy named Kevin Brockman stopped by. At first I was lost. I asked her what he looked like. She described him as handsome, clean cut, brown skin, tall, and an athletic build. I knew exactly who she was talking about then.

I called him and told him what happened. Of course he already knew. I was a little shocked because he was from the Eastside, but people run their mouths so much. Our state was only but so big, everybody knew each other some way. He wanted to know where I was. I told him I would be staying with my sister for a while. He wanted to know if he could come chill. I asked Kat. She was fine with it. Since then he had been coming to visit like two or three times a week. He took me to the movies and out to dinner a few times. Kevin was the perfect gentlemen, he never tried anything.

Spinx was back around the way, looking for me of course. Caree called me about two weeks ago and told me he had threatened to have her jumped on if she didn't call.

He got on the phone demanding to know where I was. I didn't feel like arguing so I told him I was with my sister. He told me I better have my ass back home or it was going to be a problem. I hung up the phone. Needless to say, I begged Kat to take me around the way. She wasn't too happy about it, but she dropped me off at the Wawa.

I called Spinx and he picked me up. I thought we were going to Ms. Nett's, but he took me to the Courtyard Marriott instead. I didn't understand why we couldn't just go to his mom's. I missed her and wanted to see everyone. He told me it was still hot, and he didn't want me around all that nonsense.

The next day he asked if I was going to my mom's. I told him he could drop me off at the bus stop, I would catch the bus to my sisters. He didn't argue, he gave me a few hundred and sat with me until the bus came. I stayed with him a few more times since then.

Last night was one of them.

When we first pulled up to the Elms Apartment complex, thoughts of what Kat said about him living with his other woman popped up. My whole body began to tense up and I felt nauseous. Spinx must have felt my vibe; he gave me a quick kiss on the lips. He parked the Honda Wagon, turned the car off and turned to me.

"You know I love you, right?" he asked while rubbing my thigh.

I slowly nodded while looking out the side window. I already didn't like the way this was going. I took a deep breath to prepare myself for whatever he was about to say.

To my surprise he didn't say anything more. He got out the car, came over to my side and opened the door. I grabbed my overnight bag and followed him to the building.

The apartment was on the first floor. He pulled his keys out of his coat pocket, smiling at me while he opened the door. Once inside the first thing I noticed was Kita sitting at a glass and onyx dining room table. In front of her sat a big bowl of home fried chicken, macaroni and cheese, collard greens and fresh biscuits. My mouth began to water at the sight of it. She was sitting there smiling with this oversized T-shirt and a pair of sweat pants on. It looked like she'd picked up a few pounds. Looking at all the food on the table I could see why. Spinx grabbed my bag and sat it on the side of the plush brown couch. He then held my hand and seated me at the table next to Kita. He sat in front of both of us and started digging in the food.

I sat there confused; not really knowing what the hell was going on. Kita grabbed a plate without saying a word to me or giving me any real eye contact since I walked through the door. I looked around the apartment and checked it out. It was cute, nothing like Ms. Nett's or Kat's. Everything looked like it came from Riverwine Furniture. The kind of stuff you need to replace in six months, nothing to brag about. I started to feel a few cramps in my pelvic area. I guess Spinx noticed the discomforting look on my face and asked what was wrong.

"You ok?" he asked, putting the fork down.

I rubbed my hand over my stomach. I didn't answer.

Spinx picked up a plate and handed it to Kita. She stopped eating and immediately began to pile food on the plate. When she was finished she sat the plate in front of me and continued to eat. I didn't know what type time they were on or what this was supposed to be, but I damn sure wasn't feeling this whole *family* scene at all.

"Spinx, what the fuck is going on here? Why you got me up in this bitch's house? I didn't forget that you were fucking this bitch and that dirty bitch Shay! I know you ain't think shit was cool because we fuckin' again!" I looked at Kita to see how she would react to the news of me and Spinx being back together. To my surprise she didn't even flinch. She acted like she didn't even hear how I just totally disrespected her in her crib.

Spinx looked at me and smiled. "Baby, Kita is family, she knows how you feel about what happened and she's sorry. We just want to make things right for our kids. Nyse, be a sweetheart and let the past be the past. We're starting over with a clean slate. Tell her Kita, we a family and you're not out to hurt her."

Kita grabbed my hand. I quickly snatched it away. "Nyse, I am not trying to come between you and Braxton. He really loves you… and so do I. He is my *best friend*, and I'll do *anything* for him. When he's hurt so am I. I am so sorry if I offended you in any way. You know if you stress yourself too much you can stress the baby. Please forgive me." Kita had a sincere look in her eyes.

I guess she was really sorry. Plus, if Spinx was really into her like that he would have never bought me here. I couldn't be mad anyway, it's not like I hadn't been stuck up Kevin's ass the last few weeks. I gave her a half-ass smile and took a bite of the food, which was awesome.

After dinner Spinx took me to *his* room and Kita stayed behind to clean up. I noticed that his room had nothing in it but a dresser with a twenty-seven inch TV and a queen size mattress, which was sitting on the floor. He kicked off his Tims and undressed until he was in nothing but his boxers. I undressed too, but kept my panties and bra on. Regret hit me as soon as my skin touched the sheets. They felt real gritty, like they hadn't been washed in a minute. He pulled me closer to him and I lay my head on his chest.

"You enjoy yourself tonight?" he asked.

"Yes, dinner was really good."

"That's good… look, tomorrow my family is having a get together for Memorial Day in Denton. I thought you may have wanted to go, but I noticed you've been having pains and shit. So I think maybe you should stay behind."

I agreed with him. I couldn't go even if I wasn't having the pains. I had plans of my own and he wasn't included.

Chapter 7
VENGEANCE IS MINE

Caree was in the kitchen making Kool-Aid. I was lying on the couch. I had been feeling funny all morning. I was cramping in my pelvic area and back. It almost felt like I was coming on my period, or had to take a serious shit. I lay there moaning and rocking back and forth. Caree came in with two cups in her hands.

"Here, girl, I made the *red* kind like you requested," she said.

I was in too much pain to respond. Tears escaped from the corner of my eyes, and I bit down on my lip.

She sat next to me. Her tone changed from joke mode to concerned, "Nyse, you all right?"

At this point I couldn't hold it any longer. I let out an excruciating moan. It felt like my insides were being ripped apart.

She began to panic. "What happened? Did someone call and upset you?"

I knew she couldn't be serious. There was no way I would be carrying on like this from a phone call. I managed to speak. "My stomach is killing me. I need to shit, and it's not coming out."

"Whatever you do, Nyse, don't push. I'm calling the ambulance!" she said, as she ran to the phone and called an ambulance.

I sat up on the couch rocking back and forth, praying for the pain to stop. When she hung up the phone I ordered her to call Spinx. The doorbell rang, and Caree hurried to the door. A few seconds later she was accompanied by Kevin and his boy Roc. I was a little bugged out because Kevin didn't know I was pregnant. My intentions were to tell him today but it was too late. Caree and her big mouth had already filled him in on everything. To my surprise it didn't seem to be an issue, because he held me in his arms. The last thing I remember was him telling me everything was going to be all right, before everything went black.

•••••••••••••••••••••••••••••••••

I opened my eyes and everything was a blur. I tried to sit up, but the heaviness I was feeling wouldn't allow me to move. I looked around the room and noticed I was in a hospital. I was confused. I looked to my left and saw Caree. Everything started to make more sense. I looked around the room for Spinx, but he was nowhere to be found.

"What happened... why do I feel so drugged? I know I ain't having the damn baby this early?"

Caree held her head down and looked away. I noticed a single tear slide down her cheek. I knew what was up. She didn't even have to say a word.

"I lost it, didn't I?

She shook her head sympathetically and said, "Yes."

I closed my eyes and asked God *why*. I didn't deserve this. This was going to mess everything up. I *needed* that baby;

that was the only way I could really have the upper hand with Spinx. I would have something those other bitches didn't… his child. Now that was done, what was I to do now? In the middle of my pity party the door opened. A slender, medium height man, dressed in hospital scrubs, walked in. He asked Caree to leave the room. Once she was out of sight he turned to me with a fake smile.

"Ms. Nyse, my name is Dr. Brown, and I am sorry to tell you that you had something we call a mis-abortion...."

I was pissed. "Abortion... I didn't have any abortion." I didn't like the tone he was using with me. He acted like I wasn't shit, just another statistic.

He gave me a weak smile and said, "No, honey... the baby aborted itself. This happens when there is an infection or the baby isn't developing properly. It's a form of miscarriage. Did you know that you were carrying Chlamydia? We believe that's what caused the miscarriage."

I thought I was about to vomit when the word "Chlamydia" came from his arrogant mouth. "Oh my GOD!" I cried. I put my hands over my face, I was so embarrassed.

Dr. Brown scribbled something down on the clipboard he was holding. "Well, we treated you for it, and I will give you a prescription so you can continue to take the pills. You need to let your sex partner or partners know what's going on, so *they* don't re-infect you... and Ms. Nyse, you really should practice safe sex so this doesn't happen again. You can get your clothes on, and your gentlemen friend is outside waiting for you."

Dr. Brown gave me a pat on the leg, handed me the prescription and was out the door. I was so mad that I didn't know what to do. I couldn't believe how he was judging me. I'd only slept with one person in my life! I bit my lip to stop myself from screaming. I couldn't believe that bastard burnt me. I'd lost my baby because of him being trifling. All the love I had for Spinx had crept out the door. He was going to pay for this. I couldn't believe he had the nerve to show his black face up here.

When the door opened I prepared myself to cuss that black bastard out. Instead Kevin walked in with balloons and a long box with a big red bow. He handed me the box and tied the balloons to my wrist. I opened the box, which contained a mix of 12 pink, red and white long stem roses. He leaned over and gave me a hug and I bust out crying in his arms. He told me not to worry because I would be able to have more kids later. That wasn't the reason I was crying. I couldn't tell him that it was because my pussy was on fire. I had to admit, it felt good to be in his arms. I felt like I could just tell him everything, and he could make it better.

I opened my eyes and noticed Caree standing at the door. I broke my embrace with Kevin. "Did Spinx ever call you back?" I sniffled.

She looked at Kevin as if she was looking for some type of approval. He was holding my hand, but his attention was on Caree.

"Just tell her the truth," Kevin said.

She pulled up a chair alongside my bed. "Nyse, I didn't want to tell you. Today is Shay's birthday, and Spinx took her to the beach right after he dropped you off this morning."

••••••••••••••••••••••••••••••••••

I was released from the hospital later that night. Kevin took Caree back home. I wasn't feeling her after she told me that shit about Spinx. What pissed me off is that she knew the whole time he was with that raggedy bitch and she didn't tell me. I thought we were friends, but that goes to show you can't trust nobody. Kevin came back to the crib after he dropped her off. I really didn't want any company, but he insisted. I went straight to my room and left him in the den.

I had too much on my mind. I had to figure out a way for Spinx to pay for what he'd done to me. My little world was slowly crumbling down. I couldn't understand why he would do that to me, I mean, I hadn't done anything wrong. I'd done everything he wanted me to do. I lay on my bed scrutinizing this whole mess. I wonder if Shay's dad knew she was fucking a twenty-six year old; one that basically took his spot when he went to the Feds. I smiled sneakily to myself. I wondered what he would do if he knew his woman and daughter where sucking off the same man knowingly. I lay in bed contemplating on what my next move would be until I drifted off to sleep.

The next day I was bleeding like a race horse. Kevin stayed to help me out. I called my sister and told her what happened.

"Oh my God, do you want me to come home?" she sympathetically asked.

"I'm cool. Kevin is here helping me." I could tell that she was actually happy that I wasn't having the baby.

Kat snapped. "Who the hell is Kevin?" she asked.

"Kevin is Brock's real name."

She seemed to calm down. "Oh, I'm used to calling him by his street name. I'll be back late Monday night. Call me if you need me."

When I hung up Caree was calling. I didn't know what the fuck she wanted, because I wasn't dealing with her fake ass any more. I bet she was running her mouth telling everybody out the way what went down. *Bitch!* I thought.

"Hello," I said with an attitude.

"Hold on," she said returning the same attitude.

I wanted throw up when I heard the next voice.

"Baby... I'm so sorry I wasn't there for you." It was Spinx. "How did it happen? Were you not taking care of yourself right?" he said sadly.

I looked at the phone like is this fool crazy. "No, nigga, I wasn't taking care of myself right… by having sex with you RAW!" I shouted. "You gave me a fucking disease, that's what killed our baby!"

He was quiet.

"What, you ain't got shit to say now? Oh… and how was your little trip to the beach? Did you break that bitch in right? Oh, I forgot, she already loose," I said sarcastically.

"Huh?" he tried to play the dumb role. "The beach... I went with my family to the beach... break who in?" he stammered.

He was starting to really piss me off, so I decided to play stupid with him. I guess he forgot he told me he was going to Maryland. "You know what... I'm sorry... I'm just upset because you weren't there for me... when our baby died. Who gave you Chlamydia?" I asked calmly.

"Baby, I knew about the disease... I didn't think it went to you because you never said nothing about it. That bitch Kita gave it to me... but I handled that shit… I ain't fuckin' wit' her like that no more... I'm sorry... we can try again though... because I want you to have my baby," he begged.

Kita? So I guess that little speech she made at dinner was bullshit, I thought. I was getting more vexed as the minutes rolled on. I took a deep breath and continued my little game. "I know baby... we all make mistakes... and soon as I am healed we will try again." I lied.

"When can I see you?" he asked. "I miss you... and I want

to make it up to you," he said softly.

"Soon... baby, I will be back real soon," I said.

He told me he loved me and we hung up.

I got up from the bed and started packing a few outfits. I showered and dressed. I went downstairs with my bag. Kevin was playing "*Bloody Roar*" on the Play Station. I swear the only reason niggas liked that game was because the bitch's titties would bounce even when they weren't fighting.

When he noticed the bag he pause the game. "Where do you think you're going?"

I went to the closet to grab my jacket. "I need my mother, I'm going through too much and I need her."

He turned off the game and helped me with my jacket. "Are you sure you're ready to tell her about this? Don't you want to wait for your sister to come home so she can support you?"

He was full of questions that I just did not feel like answering.

"I know what I'm doing, Kevin," I assured him.

He grabbed my bag and we were on our way.

My mom wasn't home as usual, and by the looks of it she hadn't been home for days. Kevin helped me in the house with my bags.

"Do you want me to stay here with you?" he asked.

"No. You've done enough. Go and have some fun, I'll be fine," I said.

He was about to walk out the door, and I grabbed his arm. I gave him a big hug and then kissed him gently on the lips. He pressed me up against him and slipped his tongue in my mouth. We kissed intensely, forever. At least it seemed that way. I pulled away when I felt his erection rise against my stomach.

"Kevin, I want you to come to my graduation and afterwards I want you to be with me," I said.

"What about Spinx?" he asked.

"He don't matter to me no more," I said. A sly smile spread across my face. "I doubt if he'll be around anyway... I'll call you tomorrow."

He gave me a quick peck and walked to his Range Rover. I smiled as he started his truck. *Damn, he's fine and he's paid,* I thought. *He would be a great replacement for Spinx*. I watched him drive down the street.

Chapter 8
THE SET UP

I went to my room and changed into an all black Gap sweat suit. I patiently sat on my bed and watched the clock. When the time was right, I put my Polaroid camera in my bag. I took a deep breath and sighed. I closed my eyes and thought everything over. I had to do this for me. I was tired of being the victim. Shit was about to hit the fan. I grabbed my bag and left the house.

It was dark as shit walking through those paths, but I knew them like the back of my hand. I knew damn well that I shouldn't have been out and walking down a damn hill that soon after the miscarriage, but I was on a mission. When I reached Ms. Netts I sat across the street on the green box and watched her house and Meekie's. They were only a few houses apart, and I knew I was going catch some type of action.

I pulled out my camera and waited for shit to pop off. Like ten minutes later I saw a few customers come up. I took their pictures and pictures of their license plates. I saw a bunch of grown ass men come from Meekie's with her Young Girl Crew and take them to Ms. Netts. I snapped that too. I thought maybe I shouldn't bring everybody down, because I was just after Spinx. I thought about it and quickly changed my mind. They shouldn't be fucking with those young girls anyway, serves them right. I'd had enough of the outside action so I crept around back.

Killa, their pit, was outside, but he knew my scent. He came running over to me with his tongue hanging out wanting to play. I patted his head and told him to sit. He obeyed. I peeped through the back window and no one was in the kitchen. I used my key and went through the back door.

I opened up the cabinet in the kitchen and opened a secret compartment, just as I expected, *Jackpot.* I took pictures of the coke and heroine they had up in there. I peeked around the corner to see if anyone was in the living room. A few members of his squad were there, but they were knocked out drunk. I heard that Spinx threw a big neighborhood barbeque earlier that day. I knew they were tore up and would be out cold.

I tiptoed up the steps. I heard noises coming from the Hilton. I crept the door open and peeked in. I saw the usual, old ass men fucking those young girls from Meekie's. I snapped a few pictures; they were so into their groove that they didn't even notice the flash. *Perverts,* I thought. I put the camera in my purse and stood in front of Spinx's door. I put my ear to it and I heard the bed post knocking. I could hear him asking some chick if that was his pussy and of course she was yelling it was. The words he was saying was so familiar. My heart began to ache. After hearing that, I knew I was doing the right the thing. I turned away and left Ms. Nett's for the last time.

••••••••••••••••••••••••••••••••••••

The next morning I woke up eager to start phase two. I

went to the Uni-Mart to wait for Captain Oliver Brennan. I had a little package for him that would change his life forever. He was a cop who couldn't wait to bust Spinx and his boys. He was inside the little store getting his coffee. I walked pass his squad car and dropped the package in his window. I left a typed note stating that he needed to act fast before the evidence was no longer there. I hid in the cut and watched him as he retrieved the package. A few minutes later he was acting as if he'd won the lotto.

•••••••••••••••••••••••••••••••

I couldn't believe that in just a few hours I would be a high school graduate. Everyone was gathered at my mom's before the ceremony. I was on the phone with Spinx. He'd promised me he would be at the graduation. I'd given him a ticket the night before when he'd taken me out to dinner and surprised me with a diamond and ruby tennis bracelet.

"Let's go to the mote," he'd said.

"I'm not ready… I'm still not over the miscarriage," I told him.

He seemed a little disappointed.

"Can we go to your house? I haven't seen Ms. Nett in a minute," I asked him.

"Umm… she at… her sister's house," he stuttered as if he was lying.

When we pulled up to my mom's house he leaned over for a kiss but stopped. Something in the driveway caught his attention. I turned my head and stared towards my driveway. I didn't see anything unusual.

"What are you looking at?" I'd inquired.

"Yo, wassup with you and Brock? Why whenever I hear your name his follows it up?" he asked.

I followed his gaze and noticed him staring at Brock's Range Rover in my driveway.

A mischievous smile crept on my face. "Oh... Kevin... he's my friend. He just seems to be there when I need him... like after the *party*, and when I *lost* our baby. He was right there to comfort me." I rubbed it in.

He shifted his body towards his window. "Comfort you... what you mean comfort you... and he let you call him by his government?" he said, sounding heated.

I made things even worse. "Yeah, he said he didn't want me calling him by his street name. Said I was different than the other chicks, and I deserved the right to call him Kevin."

I studied his facial expression and was satisfied at the repulsive look he wore. He didn't like that shit at all. I leaned over and kissed his face.

As I was getting out the car I said, "You don't have to take me to my hair appointment tomorrow, Kevin is taking me after we go pick up my cell phone." Before he could say a word I slammed the door and ran to the house. He was vexed. *And to think, this is just the beginning,* I thought.

I wrapped up my call with Spinx and got ready to go to my graduation. Two days had passed since my attempt to set him up. To my surprise nothing had happened. To be honest, it seemed like the cops just disappeared. They weren't sitting in the cars at the park like they usually did, nor where they in their office in the neighborhood community center. I just hoped that my plan wouldn't fold. Spinx needed to be taught a lesson.

••••••••••••••••••••••••••••••••••••

Vice-Principal Scott announced into the microphone, "Nalyse Lynae Nyse."

I walked across the stage and was handed my diploma. I waved to my cheering squad in the stands. I heard a few boo's, but then I heard Ra-Ra and his boys whistling and screaming my name. My mom was crying. Kat and Kevin were clapping and cheering.

Just then I heard, "THAT'S RIGHT, GET THAT DIPLOMA FOR DADDY!" I turned to the opposite direction and noticed Spinx and his flunkies. I didn't even acknowledge him.

"He's such a fuckin' jerk," I said under my breath. I hoped my mother didn't hear his ignorant ass. She still didn't know I was dealing with him.

I sat there as everyone made their boring speeches. My stomach was in knots. I was happy that this chapter of my life was going to finally be over. I felt bad when everybody were hugging each other and crying. Nobody even looked in my direction. I'd really fucked up my high school career socially. Maybe I would do better in college. Getting in would be no problem, I'd maintained a 3.0 average. I noticed my flirt buddy Dale. He didn't even come over and congratulate me. He was too busy slobbing down some blonde. I didn't even bother to throw my cap up with everyone else. I sat in the hard steel chair waiting for the bullshit to be over.

All of the graduates rushed out to meet their families in the lobby. They were taking pictures with each other. I found my mom and the crew. My mom was chatting with her sisters smiling from ear to ear. We were all happy; they wanted to take pictures with me. I took a few with them. I was standing next to one of my little cousins when I felt a tap on the shoulder. I turned around and was in heaven.

Standing before me was Rashawn, looking like an angel in his white Armani Exchange linen outfit. It really complemented his smooth flawless toffee brown skin. He handed Kat the camera and asked her to take a picture of us. She seemed to have a little attitude, but did it anyway. Ra-Ra put his arms around me, like we were an item or something. I began to sweat and my heart was beating a mile a minute. I hadn't felt like that since the night of E's party.

"I bet you like that. All hugged up with my man," Kat mumbled.

I was about to respond until I noticed Kevin rushing towards us. Soon as the camera flashed Ra-Ra pushed me to the floor. *Pop... pop...* I heard people screaming. Two more shots followed. That's when I saw the rest of Ra-Ra's crew come out of nowhere busting their guns. Everyone was running and screaming. This was Déjà vu like a mutha fucka. I couldn't find my mom and sister. I was on the floor crawling around looking for them. I looked to the left and saw one of my classmates lying on the floor with blood leaking from his body. *Oh God... please let me make it out of here. Let my family be ok,* I thought. I felt someone lift me by my waist. I looked up, and it was Kevin.

I screamed, "We can't leave... we can't leave without my family!" I was trying to fight him off me as we made our way through the crowd.

Once outside, he pulled me along as we ran to his truck. He pushed me in the back, then jumped in and sped off. I tried to get out, but he had the safety lock on.

"Let me the FUCK out!" I kicked the car doors screaming.

His cell phone rang and I heard him say, "I got her in the car with me... she's all right... ok... ok... SAY WORD! All right then... will do."

I climbed in the front seat. "Who... was that?" I asked anxiously.

"Your sister and mom is cool... they are headed to your sister's crib."

"What about Ra-Ra, is he ok?" I asked.

"I think so... you know he had a vest on. But your boy Spinx... shit ain't too pretty for him right now. I just heard from someone that they have the whole Serenity Hills blocked off. The State boys, County, and the DEA are running through his mom's house and a few other cribs as we speak," he said in disbelief.

I sat back in the seat and exhaled. A little smile of relief and satisfaction spread across my face. I didn't expect a shootout to happen, but everything was going as planned.

••••••••••••••••••••••••••••••••

Complete chaos is how you would describe the scene at Kat's. My mom was hysterical. Mr. Dave was trying to calm her down. The phone was ringing off the hook. Everyone was on their cell phones checking to see if there were any fatalities from the shooting. My family from out of town was really shook up.

My aunt Sarah was talking trash to my mom. "Kat's boyfriend is a hoodlum and it's your fault. You put your job and Mr. Dave before your own kids. They don't have proper supervision, that's why they're both messing with drug dealers, and your son is in jail."

My mom cried as she took a verbal lashing from her older sister. Mr. Dave tried to defend her, but Aunt Sarah shot him down too. I wasn't trying to get involved. Arguing with Aunt Sarah was a no-win situation.

I slipped through the crowd in search of Kat. I found her in the basement. She was whispering on the phone to someone. I sat on the leather love seat and waited for her to finish her conversation. After a few minutes she noticed she wasn't alone and ended the call. Her eyes were puffy and her face was red. She had been crying.

"You ok?" she asked.

"I'm fine. How about you? Have you heard from Ra-Ra?" I asked.

She took a deep breath and sat back on the couch. "Yeah, he only has a little flesh wound on the shoulder."

Kat seemed a little disappointed by that. *Damn, did she want the nigga to die?* I thought. We sat in silence. She got up from her seat and walked over to a wall beside the stairs. I watched her grab a small key like object from under the third step. She took the object and ran it along the edge of the wood panel and a little door opened. She pulled a little brown envelope from the opening and closed it. She handed me the envelope and sat back down.

From my expression I knew she figured I was at a complete loss. The envelope reminded me of the ones they gave you at your local bank. She told me to open it. I had to admit; with all that was going on I was afraid to look in it. I opened it up and there were a set of car keys. I held the keys in my hand. I thought they were an extra set to her Lexus. I looked at Kat for an explanation, and she told me to go look in the garage. A half smile spread across her face.

I know this is not what I think it is, I thought. I ran upstairs to the garage. I hurried through the house so quick I didn't even pay attention to the fact that my mom and Aunt Sarah were toe to toe, ready to get it on. I opened the garage door and before my eyes sat a brand new 1996 Nissan Pathfinder. I was so siked. I opened the doors to smell the new car fragrance. The interior had cream leather seats with wood grain on the dash. I jumped in and cranked the engine. I had to check out the Pioneer stereo system. It was bangin'.

Kat banged on the window. I rolled it down to thank her. "Girl, are you crazy? Are you trying to kill yourself and every damn body else?" she yelled.

At first I didn't catch on to what she was talking about. Then I was like. "Ohhh... Carbon monoxide." I was so hyped about my new whip, I forget all about being in a closed-in space. I turned the truck off.

When I got out I gave Kat a big hug.

"It's a graduation present from me and Rashawn," she told me.

"Let me use your phone so I can call and thank him."

She rolled her eyes and sucked her teeth. "You can't call him right now. He's being questioned at the police station about the shooting. They are trying to see if he knew who would want to kill him," she said.

Damn! I was so into my gift that I forgot my graduation had just turned into a bloodbath. I had a quick flashback of the event.

"Does he know who it was?" I asked.

She shook her head no and quietly walked in the house. I followed behind her.

In the living room my mom was gathering her things. Aunt Sarah and her crew were already gone.

"Wow! They got out of here awfully quick," I said.

Mr. Dave gave me a hug and handed me a card. "Your mom and I are really proud of you."

I went over to my mom, who was fiddling with her purse.

"You ok?"

She didn't answer. I noticed that her face was stained with tears. I felt so bad. This was supposed to be a great day, but it turned out to be a complete mess. I tried to talk to her, but she continued to ignore me. I felt myself getting a little agitated. Mr. Dave was talking to Kat when he noticed how my mother was acting towards me. I grabbed her arm.

"Mom... what is your problem? Did I do something to upset you?" I asked.

She looked into my eyes. Tears began to fall from hers. Without saying a word she grabbed her jacket and walked out the door. I looked at Kat for answers. She shrugged her shoulders and walked away.

Mr. Dave gave me a hug. "Nalyse, she's ok, she's just shook up from the shooting. She came so close to losing both you and Rashawn. You know how much she cares for the young man. Of course the shouting match she had with Sarah didn't help. Give her time, she'll be ok." He kissed my cheek and left the house.

In the beginning I'd had my doubts about Mr. Dave, but I guess he really did love my mom. I peeped out the window and watched them get in the car. I was relieved to see it wasn't me she was mad at. Mr. Dave was trying to talk to her, but she didn't respond to him either.

Oh well, I thought. *I'll call her in the morning to check on her*. I shut the blinds and walked over to the dining room table. I grabbed up a few chips and a piece of cake. I enjoyed my little snack while I envisioned Spinx's reaction when he found out he was being raided. I laughed to myself. *That's what his ass gets. I mean, I know he ain't think I was gonna let him play me like that. Not me. Not Ms. Nyse. I'm young, but I'm no damn fool, well, at least I'm not a fool anymore*, I thought. I picked up the phone to check on Kevin, but his answering machine picked up. I left a message and hung up.

I went upstairs to change my clothes. On my way back down the stairs I heard the doorbell. I ran to get it, hoping it was Kevin. When I opened the door there stood a tall, brown skin brother. He had to be at least 6'4. He had a nice frame; he wasn't all tall and lanky. His face was pretty. I mean, he seemed to be overly well kept for a man. For a minute I thought he arched his damn eyebrows.

"You must be Nalyse? Kat has told me so much about you." His voice was smooth.

He walked pass me into the house. Kat came up from the basement and wrapped her arms around the man's neck. They shared a long passionate kiss. She looked over at me and winked and they went upstairs. I was disgusted.

I can't believe her. Somebody just tried to take Ra's life and she got the nerve to invite another man in his house, I thought. She didn't deserve him. If he was with me I would've been at that police station with him, holding him down. I had to get out of there. I wished Ra-Ra would just pop up and see that shit. That would knock that bitch right off her throne. I decided I would go tell Rashawn thank you in person. But first I wanted to go to the Hills and show off my new ride.

I called my girl Kee from my new cell phone to see if she wanted to hang out. There was no answer. I wondered if she was all right. She was about due any day now. I decided to ride pass her apartment to check on her. Ten minutes later I pulled in front of her complex. I looked up at her windows. It seemed to be extra dark in there. The light from the TV would usually be glowing.

I climbed the stairs to apartment 2-C. I rang the door bell, but no one answered. I knocked a few times before I turned away. As I was going down the stairs I heard someone calling my name. I walked back towards the apartment. Kee's younger sister Michelle was at the top of the stairs. She was holding little Myia on her hip. I figured Kee must have went into labor since her sister had the baby. I followed her into the apartment. The place was ransacked. The couches were cut open; everything was pulled out of the cabinets and thrown on the floor. It looked as if a cyclone hit the place.

"What the hell happened in here? Where's your sister?" I couldn't believe that she would leave a thirteen year old in this hell hole with her child.

Michelle placed Myai in her walker and sat on the floor next to her. "Kee got locked up down the Hill earlier. She was dropping a pack off to Ms. Nett."

Dropping a pack off... I know damn well Bo ain't have her making no runs in her condition, I thought.

"Michelle, where's Bo?"

"He's in jail too. A bunch of policemen ran up in here and took him and Co-Co. My-My and me was next door at my friend's house when it happened."

I stood there bug-eyed. I know damn well she ain't say Co-Co was up in here. "Co-Co... what the fuck… she was here? I asked.

"Yeah, she lives here now. She's Kee-Kee best friend."

Best friend? Didn't she know Co-Co was fucking her man? Bo... I thought he whooped her ass, why did he have the bitch in his house? I thought. "Get you and the baby's things together. I can't let y'all stay in this apartment. I'll get y'all a room for a few days," I said.

It was partially my fault Kee got arrested anyway. I guess I didn't think of the other people it could affect when I set Spinx up. I had a few hundred dollars I'd collected from my graduation party. I knew a thirteen year old shouldn't be in a hotel alone, but that was the only alternative they had. Their mom was strung out on dope so she wouldn't be any good to them. I couldn't take them to Kat's, she would snap. I carried Myia and her car seat to my truck.

Michelle's eyes lit up when she saw my ride. "Oh my God! This is tight! Who bought you this, Uncle Spinx?"

I burst out laughing. "Yeah right!" I lied and told her my new man bought it. I could tell that threw her off a bit.

I helped her put the bags in the trunk. Then I made sure everyone was buckled in before I pulled off. I looked back at Myia. She was so cute with her little chocolate self. She was dozing off.

"Y'all eat anything?" I asked Michelle.

"The baby did, but I'm hungry."

I thought for a moment before saying, "Nothing is open but Wawa and 7-Eleven."

"I want a hoagie so we can go to Wawa," said Michelle.

I checked into the Travelodge on New Castle Ave. I paid for three days and gave Michelle a couple dollars so they could eat.

"Call me on my cell if y'all need anything," I said.

"Thanks, Lyse."

I got back in the truck and headed towards the city. I had to admit, I was a little scared going on the Westside. I had made so many enemies. Then there was the attempt on Ra's life earlier today. I knew they thought Spinx had something to do with it. I decided to check out the police station first. I rode around the precinct and didn't see Ra's car. I pulled into a parking spot on the side of the building. I dialed his number, and to my surprise he picked up on the first ring.

"Hey, Rashawn, this is Nyse... I mean Nalyse."

"I know who it is. What's up, lil' sis?" he said.

"Umm, I'm by the police station looking for you." I thought about it for a minute and added, "I need to talk to you about something really important."

He told me to meet him at the train station, which was

right around the corner. I drove around the station a few times trying to find a parking space. It was useless; I would have to park across the street at the bus station. I tried to avoid having to go there, because I would have to parallel park and I didn't know how. I really had no reason to learn. I lived in the suburbs. I was use to pulling into a driveway.

Oh well, I thought. I guess I had no choice but to try. I found a spot and attempted to squeeze the truck into the space. It wasn't working. I noticed that a line of impatient motorist had begun to form behind me. Beads of sweat began to appear on my head. I was becoming frustrated. A few people began to shout obscenities out the window and blow their horns. I was about to roll my window down and curse them out when I heard my passenger door open. My heart almost jumped out of my chest.

"Damn, Ra! You scared the hell out of me!"

Rashawn was smiling, showing his pearly whites. He told me to relax and guided me as I pulled into the spot. I took my time and followed his direction. It turned out to be really easy. I turned the car off and took a deep breath. I had to admit, I felt a little awkward being in the car with him. I mean, if Spinx knew that I was with him he would swear I gave him information to set him up. His phone began to ring. He looked at the number, shook his head and pushed the end call button. He flashed me another smile.

"What's up, Nalyse? What you doing up here in the city? I thought you didn't get down with us like that?" He was making fun of me.

"Oh be quiet, Ra-Ra, I came up here to thank you in person for my graduation gift." I hugged him.

When I tried to let go he held on a little longer. He smelled so good, just like Fahrenheit. It made me think of Kevin, because he always wore that fragrance. Finally, he let me go.

"I really appreciate the truck. So, are you ok? Do you know who tried to kill you?" I asked bluntly. I wanted to know if he thought it was Spinx and his crew.

He sat back in his seat. "You know what? I don't even know. It got me fucked up in the head. I know it wasn't your boy Spinx. He had already left before the shooting. I heard them boys ran through the whole Hills, just about everybody got knocked."

I put my head down in shame.

You ok, Nalyse?" he asked. He looked down at me.

I forced tears from my eyes. "I don't know what to do now that Spinx is gone. He took care of me. I mean, he did his dirt. He cheated on me, gave me a disease and even had chicks he fucked approach me. Despite all that, he still took care of me." I placed my head on the steering wheel and sobbed out loud.

A concerned look covered his face. He pulled me closer to him.

"You know what's really messed up? My best friend is nine months pregnant and she's in jail. She got busted today with Spinx and them, and there's nothing I can do for her. The little money I did have I used it to put her little sister and baby in the motel for a few days. I wanted to take them to the house with me, but Kat would snap. With them there her little friend can't come over for a nightcap."

I jumped from his arms and put my hand over my mouth. "Oh my God, I didn't mean to say that." I studied his face to see if he'd caught what I said. He must not have heard me, because he continued his conversation.

"You know he thinks Brock did it. He thinks he did it to get him out the picture so he can get at you. I heard there was a little gun play between a few of his boys and Brock. I'm still waiting to hear from him now. No one has heard from him since earlier. As for your girl, don't worry, I'll help you get her a good lawyer. She'll get off and be able to keep her kids. We can go to the station and see what her bail is. And as for her sister, I will give you some money to look after them for a minute." He paused and turned towards the window. "So, Kat be entertaining niggas in my crib, huh?"

I sat up. "No... I didn't mean that, not niggas. I mean, not a bunch of them, just one in particular." I didn't mean to tell on my sister, but I couldn't lie to him after all he was ready to do.

"You know what, I can't even be mad at her. I have a few chicks on the side myself. I mean, that's my wife right there, and I would never bring any of those bitches to my house. I mean, she could at least take the nigga to a hotel. Is he anyone I know?" he asked.

"No, he's a lame. Some college dude. He's nobody for you to worry about."

He reached for my hand. He interlocked our fingers together. I felt a little twitch between my thighs. I had to calm myself before the feeling became too intense.

"Thanks for looking out. I mean, I kind of figured she might have been steppin' out on me, but not in my crib. I knew you were thorough. I need a chick like you by my side; a chick who knows how to get as grimy as her dude when needed. Too bad you Kat's little sister. I might have taken you under my wing. Who knows, maybe you could have even taken her place," he said.

I couldn't believe what I was hearing. Was Ra-Ra trying to come on to me? I began to blush. I playfully punched him in the arm. "Yeah right, there is no way you would leave Kat alone. Queen Kat got you open. You wouldn't know what to do without her." I wanted to see where his head was really at.

His smile fell from his face, and he became serious. He

gently moved my face towards his and placed his thick lips over mine. He slipped his tongue into my mouth. I wanted to move away, but something just wouldn't let me budge. He kissed me deeply, with so much passion. He moved down to my neck and gave me little love bites. I was lost in lust. My body began to tingle, and I let go. I guess he had me where he wanted me, because he stopped. My panties were soaked. *So much for self-control,* I thought. My eyes pleaded for him to come back and finish what he'd started.

"My bad, I'm so sorry, Nalyse… I just got out of control. I mean, you actually care about me. You went against your own blood to look out for me. Not too many people would do that. I guess that turned me on. I mean, that and the fact that you're so beautiful, and your body is just right. I always knew that you would be a heartbreaker. You have so much potential. Spinx is a lucky man... I would have never treated you like he did."

He was gassing me up, and I was falling for it.

"Look, let me give you this money for your girl. I need to go before I do something I might regret," he said looking away.

He went in his pocket and pulled out a knot of money and handed it to me. I opened it and there were nothing but hundreds. He looked at me one more time before he reached for the door. His eyes showed how much he wanted me. I couldn't front, I never really looked at Ra liked that, but I wanted him, too. He had money, power and respect. Plus, he was a sharp nigga, stayed fly all the time. He started to open the door, and I grabbed his hand.

"Ra, don't leave me," I said in a seductive voice. "How about we go somewhere so we can discuss how I can be number one in your life." I couldn't believe what I was saying.

Ra smiled. He kissed me on the lips and told me to get a

room at the Courtyard Hotel on Washington Street. He said he would meet me there in a half an hour, because he had to take care of some business first. After he got out the car he tapped on my window. I rolled it down.

"Nalyse, are you sure about this? If we do this there is no turning back, and I'm not sharing you with any other nigga, you understand?"

I shook my head yes.

He walked across the street and hopped on his midnight blue Suzuki GSXR1100. I watched as he put on his matching helmet and sped off. I pulled out of the parking spot. *I'll be riding on the back of that bike soon,* I thought.

Just that quick, I had forgotten all about Kevin. I still cared about him, but I had to push those feelings aside. This was an opportunity I just couldn't let pass me by. All those Westside bitches would be worshipping me in a minute. God knows this was not what I planned to happen. I was beaming on the inside. Fuck a Queen Kat, Nyse would be the Queen Bitch now.

••••••••••••••••••••••••••••••••

Wow was all I could say. Ra-Ra could really put it down in bed. I'd thought Spinx was something. I felt guilty at first. I was about to leave out the room before he got there, but it was too late. When I opened the door he was standing there smiling, looking all fine. His smooth skin looked good enough to eat. I thought I would get some cavities before I had a chance to even taste it. I couldn't quite understand why Kat would even fathom cheating on this nigga. He was amazing and so sweet it was ridiculous.

He gently laid me across the bed and slowly removed my

clothing piece by piece, tasting every part of my body. He licked between my toes and everything. Unlike Spinx, he was not a talker, nor was he aggressive, in the beginning. It wasn't until the end when he really put it on me. He had me running from the dick. When I finally couldn't take any more, he ejaculated inside of me. Of course I didn't think anything of it; I was so lost in lust. He climbed off top of me and held me while we talked about our future.

"Rashawn, do you think I'm a bad person? I mean, Kat is my sister, and I just violated her in the worst way." I knew it was too late to feel bad now. The deed was done, and I honestly didn't plan to stop being with Rashawn as long as he was cool with it.

"You know what… I actually admire the fact that you're not afraid to get what you want. I had a little crush on you for a minute now. I knew it was wrong because you were my girl's sister. I just didn't know you felt the same way until that night under the light pole." He winked and smiled.

I pulled the covers over my face in embarrassment. "Was I that obvious?" I said shyly.

He playfully snatched the covers from my face. "Yes, you were *that* obvious. But it's cool. If it wasn't for the fact that all hell was breaking loose I probably would have scooped you up that night."

He leaned over and kissed my forehead and pulled me close to his naked body.

We talked about the babies that Kat aborted and how he'd really wanted them He told me that he'd promised to leave the street life alone if she had them. I met another side of Ra-Ra. I met Rashawn Gibbs. He wasn't that cold hearted nigga everyone in the streets feared. He just wanted a family.

He made me promise to leave Spinx and if I was interested in Brock to cut ties with him. He assured me in time that

I was going to be his woman and bare his children. I felt so safe and relaxed in his arms. It felt like everything was about to come together for me. We discussed my schooling. I told him my dream of becoming a lawyer. He told me that he had family that worked at University of Maryland Eastern Shore. He said it would be easier for us to spend time with each other if I went there first and we could eventually venture to D.C. so I could attend Georgetown.

It was too good to be true. I began to wonder if he was trying to gas my head up so he could have access to the pussy. He must have read my mind, because he promised me that in time Kat would be out the picture, but he just needed to do it the right way. He admitted that he still loved her. I understood; they had been together since eighth grade. I knew his feelings wouldn't leave over night. He assured me that spending more time with me would help him get his mind off of her.

The next morning his phone was ringing off the hook. He was still sleep. I leaned over him and peaked at the number. It was Kat. I began to feel nauseous. I looked at Rashawn laying there ass naked. I felt a lump in my throat. *Damn, Nyse… you done fucked up again. What kind of person would fuck her sister's man?* I thought. I nudged Rashawn to wake him up. He didn't budge. I began to get paranoid. *What if someone told her we are together? I mean, the city ain't that big and everyone knows everybody. What if one of her friends works here at the hotel?* I thought.

I ran to the window and peeked out the blinds. I searched for something familiar, but didn't see anything. The phone began to ring again. It was Kat; she was blowing his phone up. This time Rashawn heard it and answered. He spoke to her very calmly. I heard her yelling through the phone.

"She's probably hanging with her friends baby… come on… Kat, I don't think she's in any trouble… let me call Brock and see if she's with him. So, how was your night? I was waiting for your call." He flashed a sneaky smile at me. "Oh… you took a valium for your nerves… oh, ok, baby. Well let me get up and start my day. Will I see you for lunch? Ok… I love you too, see you later." He hung up.

I was so envious. I mocked him "I love you, too… ok, baby." I crossed my arms and rolled my eyes.

I knew I'd made a mistake. He wasn't going to leave her. Rashawn ignored my smart comment and went into the bathroom. I heard him turn the shower on. After a few moments he came out the bathroom.

"Are you going to sit on the bed and sulk like a young girl, or take care of your man?"

I sat there mad for a minute. He stood at the door waiting for me. A few seconds later I got up and went to the door. He grabbed my hand and led me into the shower. We explored each other's body again. This time he was more intense and romantic. He made love to me.

I was getting dressed, and Rashawn was on his way out.

"Look. Make sure you call your sister. Tell her you were at one of your little girl friend's house or something. Oh, call me if you need more loot to bail home girl out, just make sure you block your number. Your sister's real nosy." He gave me a kiss on my lips. "Keep the room for another night. You need a few more workouts to get our rhythm right."

I smiled as he left. Soon as he was out the door I called Kat. She tried to curse me out about not coming back home. I had to remind her that I was grown now. I told her she wasn't worried about me anyway because she had that nerd over there breaking her back in. She called me a bitch before she hung up. I smiled. *That's right Ms. Kat, you keep fucking that lame nigga while I'm concentrating on taking your place,* I thought.

Chapter 9
THE AFTERMATH

Kee had finally been released from WCI (Women's Correctional Institution). It had been five hours since I'd posted her seventy-five hundred dollar bail. I'd only had five thousand on me, so I called Ra-Ra and one of his boys brought me over three more. He couldn't do it himself because he was entertaining my sister. I was cool with that. It was only a matter of time before it would be my turn. Kee looked really bad. Her stomach was so big it looked like she was about to pop. She looked around searching for her ride. I beeped the horn and stuck my head out the window.

"I'm over here, big ass!" I joked.

She smiled and wobbled over to the truck. She slid in the passenger seat and looked around in amazement. "Is this you?" she asked.

I shook my head proudly.

"Damn. Girl, you came up. I know Spinx ain't buy this, it must have been that nigga Brock," she said as she admired my ride.

"You damn right Spinx broke ass ain't buy this, Ra-Ra bought this for me, as a graduation gift." I gloated.

You could tell she was confused. "Ra-Ra bought you this?

Are you serious? Why would your sister's boyfriend get you a brand new truck? I mean, what did your sister say?"

She had her face turned up. I was starting to feel some type of way. I was beginning to think that the green envy monster was showing himself yet again through Kee. She must have read my mind, because she changed the subject.

"So, did Bo give you the money to bail me out?" she asked sounding hopeful.

I had to bust her bubble real quick. "Hell No! He locked up with Co-Co and left your sister and the baby in that fucked up apartment. I bailed you out. Speaking of Co-Co, what the fuck is up with her? I heard that was your new *BEST FRIEND*." I had to stress that.

She sighed. "Nyse, I'm just trying to maintain. I mean, Bo got her there cleaning up and watching the baby while we make this paper. It's nothing serious, they ain't fucking no more. Well, at least not like they were. Sometimes, when I don't feel like being bothered I'm sure he knocks her off. But she knows where she stands. She'll never take my place," she explained.

She must think I am Boo-Boo the fool. This bitch has lost her damn mind. I know she ain't say they fuckin' under her damn roof, and she knows about it and accepts it, I thought. I was totally disgusted; this was not the same chick I became friends with in seventh grade. That nigga did that to her. I promised myself once I became Ra-Ra's wifey I was gonna get Kee out of that fucked up situation. She deserved better. I gave her a few dollars to get some things she needed and dropped her off at the hotel with her sister. Before I left I asked her for a favor.

"Kee, check this, I met this new guy from the city and we been kickin' it. We're not exclusive yet. I need you to cover for me tonight and any other night I need you. Kat may call you to see where I am at. Just tell her I been staying with you the last few nights, ok."

She was grinning. "I guess you are with Brock now, huh? I'm happy for you. Spinx been home with Kita more now a days. I guess he's trying to be close since she's having *another* baby. Why don't you just tell Kat? I think she would rather you be with him than Spinx."

I froze soon as she said Kita was pregnant and that she already had a child. My heart was broken. He had gotten that bitch pregnant. *That's why that bitch was wearing the baggy clothes that night at her apartment,* I thought. Then it hit me, Kee said another baby. My mind went back to when Spinx was kicking that shit about us being a family, how he wanted everything to be kosher for his kids. Then the day when Ms. Nett and I were eating breakfast, she said was I making her a grandma again. *Oh my God. They have a child together already,* I thought. *I swear I hate that nigga.* But I wasn't going to sweat it. I would most definitely have the last laugh.

"Nyse, is something wrong? You did know about Lil' Braxton, right?"

I smiled at her. "Girl, yeah, of course I did. Just do what I asked you to do for me, all right?" I pulled off before she got a chance to say anything else that would break my spirit.

••••••••••••••••••••••••••••••••••••

I was looking for something sexy to wear for Rashawn later that night. I couldn't find anything suitable. I wanted something new for my new man. I grabbed a few outfits and decided to stop by Vickie C's to get sexy for him. I ran down the stairs and bumped into Kat. She was on the phone talking to her college dude. I knew it was him because she was giggling and talking about how she enjoyed him last night. I could have kicked her. She was so stupid. She just didn't know how good she had it. *She better not try to trip when she finds out I replaced her,* I thought. She would probably thank me, since Rashawn was so bad for her. She put the phone down on her shoulder.

"Where are you going? Have you seen the news? You know your principal sent the fucking detectives to Mommy's. Thank God she wasn't there. So they had the nerve to come here questioning me about the fights you had and if I thought you were in some type of danger. Where were you all afternoon anyway? Why don't you have your phone turned on?"

I grabbed a bottle of spring water out of the fridge. I was relieved that my mother wasn't there. She would have really flipped if she found out about all that stuff that happened in school. I couldn't believe Mr. Scott thought the shooting had something to do with me. Well, at least Kat handled those detectives. At least I wouldn't have to worry about them bothering me.

"I'm staying with Kee for a few days. You know she's about to drop that load. I'm gonna watch Myai so she can rest. I might even stay with her for a few weeks. You know she's gonna need my help after the baby is born; at least until Bo gets out of jail."

She frowned. "Do you think it's a good idea to be around a new baby after you just lost yours?"

I waved her off. *Here she goes with the psychology shit*, I thought. "I'm so over that. I don't think about Spinx or that pregnancy. I'm cool. I'll call to check in."

She said something else but I wasn't trying to hear it. I walked out while she yapped away. I drove to the mall and headed straight to Vickie's. I went to the back and picked up a cute little white feathery bra and thong set. It would match well with my white feathered stiletto boots. I would be his Pocahontas for the night. Maybe we could even do a little role playing.

I stopped by the lotion and body spray display to find my Strawberries & Champagne. I loved that fragrance. I grabbed a few bottles of that and Pear and made my way to the counter. Suddenly, I literally ran into that stinkin' ass bitch Kita, of all people. I kneeled down and picked up my bottles of spray. She started helping me.

She picked up the outfit and looked at it funny. "Well, I bet Braxton would love to see you in this. What, you taking pictures to send to him or something?"

I snatched the thong from her. I looked her up and down. I noticed her belly almost immediately. "Don't you think that's your job? You're the one carrying his baby. I thought you got locked up, what you doing here?" I asked. I looked her up and down and snickered. "From the looks of it, I doubt if you could fit anything up in here anyway," I said sarcastically.

She ignored my sarcasm and smiled. "You're funny, Nyse. I did get locked up, but I was let go. Braxton told them I had nothing to do with what was going on at the house. They let me go home and they gave me *our* son back. For your information, I actually can fit something in here. I know I gained a few pounds, but that's what happens when you're six months pregnant. Maybe you'll get that far one day." She smirked.

That bitch was trying to be smart. I guess all that we are a *family* and I'm not trying to *hurt* you shit was just an act for Spinx. I wanted to spit on that bitch.

"So, would you like to go with me on Monday to see Braxton? I know he misses you. Plus we need to stick together we're all he has. Ms. Nett is pissed at him because she might lose her Section 8 and Shay is turning against him. No one knows where Spade is, it's like his ass disappeared. All his close boys have either got missing or are locked up with him. Even Brock turned against him. He set him up and then came to the Hills to act like everything was cool. That's why the young boys blew his truck up. I hope they killed that rotten mutha fucker." Her nostrils flared making her look like a pig nosed bull.

I thought my heart stopped. *Did she say they blew his truck up?* I thought. "Is Kevin ok?"

She wrinkled her nose and said nastily, "Why would you care? He set our man up. No one knows what really happened to him. When the cops got there his truck was empty. He must have escaped, but he couldn't have gotten too far. They'll probably find that nigga dead in the woods somewhere." She looked at her watch. "I gotta go, but call me on my cell if you want to go see about Braxton."

She handed me a piece of paper with her number on it. I took it and hurried to pay for my stuff. I practically ran through the mall trying to get to my truck. When I got there I bawled my eyes out. *Kevin can't be dead*, I thought.

I sat in the mall parking lot for at least an hour. People were staring as they walked by. One elderly lady knocked on my window to see if I was ok. I smiled and nodded yeah. She gave me a concerned look before leaving. I couldn't believe what was going on. I just graduated not even twenty-four hours ago. My life was changing rapidly. My head felt like it was spinning.

All of the events that had taken place kept playing over and over in my head. I tried to block out the shooting. I didn't think about turning on the news to see if any of my classmates where hurt, or even dead. I had been so busy fucking Rashawn that I forgot about Kevin. I was supposed to be with him last night. I said a quick prayer for him. I prayed that he did get away unharmed. I took a deep breath and started my truck. It was getting late; I didn't want Rashawn to think I wasn't coming.

••••••••••••••••••••••••••••••••

I lay across the bed watching reruns of "*The Facts of Life*." It was now 11 pm and Rashawn was not here. He hadn't even called to let me know what was up with him. I had bathed, put on my smell good and was waiting for him in the outfit I'd picked up earlier. I flicked the channel to see the news. The first thing that flashed on the screen was the world's drug war.

They showed Ms. Nett's house. The door was kicked in and you seen all the federal agents and local cops walking in and out of the house. Then the picture flashed over to Spinx. They had him in the cop car. You could see him yelling something at the camera. The reporter was saying he had pictures of what happened the night before, and they believed it was related to the fatal shootings at Woodrow Wilson's high school graduation.

The reporter talked about the bombing of a truck that allegedly belonged to Kevin Brockman. They found a charred body that was believed to be Brockman. He went on to say that the increase in gang violence was all connected, including the shooting and alleged murder of Brockman. He left a tip line number for anyone who had any information about the incident.

The anchor man started to talk about the notorious Braxton Hayes aka Spinx. They interviewed his former professors from Del State. They all said they were shocked, he was a promising student. They couldn't believe that he was involved in anything this repulsive. The news people called him a king pin, pimp, and pedophile. They talked about Meekie's house that was being used as a place to prostitute teenage girls. Then they showed her face on the screen. *Damn, all this because of me,* I thought. From the looks of it, Spinx was finished. I cut the television off and rolled over on my back. I let out a small scream.

"Oh my God, you scared me… again!" I was holding my chest breathing heavy.

Rashawn was standing over me wearing nothing but his award winning smile. I must have really been into the news, because I didn't even notice him come in the room. He admired my outfit.

"This is sexy, you get this for me?" he said sweetly.

I whispered, "Yes."

He massaged my thighs and pulled my legs apart. He gently lay in between them. He kissed my inner thighs. I was getting wet. I wanted him to continue, but I had to find out a few things first. I tried to sit up, but he put one of his hands on my stomach and softly pushed me back down.

"Wait a minute, Rashawn. I need to ask you a question."

He tugged at my panties to get them down. I lifted my butt off the bed so he could pull them off.

"What's up, baby?" he said. He stuck his fingers deep into my pussy and began working them.

I began to moan deeply. I caught myself from drifting away in euphoric bliss. I blurted out quickly, "Have you heard from Kevin?"

He kept massaging my girl and looked me in the eyes. "Yo, they blew that nigga's truck up. He's a goner. His peoples are losing their minds over there. . If he is that's fucked up, he was real cool. I know Fatal is going off."

I really snapped out of it. "Fatal? Why would she be going off, I didn't know she knew Kevin like that?"

He pulled his fingers out and rubbed his dick up against my soaked pussy lips. "They were real close. He didn't tell you? That's one of the reasons why no one ever fucked with him like that. Fae would merk anyone who tried to come against him. You know that's my road dawg, she is mad crazy. Not too many niggas try to fuck with her like that. You might end up dead." He pushed his dick deep into me.

I gasped.

"Now are we gonna sit and talk about Kev all night, or are you gonna give me some lovin'?"

I put my arms around his neck and pulled him down on top of me.

Around three o'clock in the morning I heard Rashawn on the phone.

"Listen, Kat, I ain't fucking nobody else… why are you trippin'? It's three in the fuckin' morning… you callin' my phone acting like some little dumb girl… no… I'm home… I'm not with no bitch. I'm at home in bed by myself… your ass should be here with me… shit has been hectic in my life and you're nowhere to be found. I love you girl… you know can't none of these females make me feel the way you can. I love Katina… I want you to be my wife but you keep telling me you ain't ready… how long you gonna make me wait? What, you trying to push me away? Baby, what you got on? Mmmmmm… that sounds good…. why don't you come to the crib? Now… right now. Ok, baby, put on one of them little skirts with no panties… yeah, throw on some heels. Don't wear no bra… I want you to walk through the door with just a skirt and those heels on, nothing else, ok? Baby, hurry up!"

He hung up the phone, jumped out the bed and put his

clothes on. I closed my eyes and pretended I was sleep. He shook me a few times.

"Nalyse, get up for minute, baby."

I acted like he interrupted my sleep. "What's wrong, Rashawn?" I said sleepily.

"Nothing... well... maybe a little something. I got to make a run real quick. You go back to sleep and I promise I'll be back first thing in the morning. I'll stop by the Post House and bring us some breakfast. We'll spend the whole day together, I promise." He kissed me and tucked me in the sheets.

I watched him walk out the door. *Lying mutha fucker*, I thought. I knew he couldn't leave her. That was all talk to get my pussy. I sat up in the bed and began to cry. I didn't understand why I couldn't just be happy. Kat was sitting here cheating on this nigga, and he still kissing her ass. What was so fucking great about her? I punched the pillow until all of my frustration was out. I refused to be a pawn in peoples little games. I was taking charge of my life.

I went over to my purse and pulled out a blunt I had tucked away. I sparked it and contemplated my next move. I was gonna make that mutha fucka eat his words. *Oh, he is gonna leave that bitch one way or the other,* I thought. He was fuckin' with the wrong bitch now.

Rashawn kept his word. He was in the bed next to me snoring. I checked the time on my cell phone. 8:30 am. I laughed to myself. *It's on now,* I thought. I ran my fingers across his bare chest and planted small kisses around his nipples. He opened one eye and smiled. I licked my lips and smiled seductively. I kissed him from his chest until I got right above his pelvis. I playfully flicked my tongue around his shaft and caressed his balls. He was really getting excited.

I continued to tease him until he begged me to taste him. I inhaled his manhood into my mouth with force. I worked my jaw muscles as I tightened my grip on his dick. I rapidly moved my tongue around as I gave him pleasure. I watched his expressions as I worked my magic. He was definitely satisfied. I had that nigga moaning my name and clawing sheets. I had to catch myself from laughing a few times. I couldn't believe the Almighty Rashawn was calling my name begging for me not to stop. I felt his dick throb, he was about to explode.

He tried to move my head. "Lyse, I'm cumin'… oh shit… I'm about to bust!"

He let loose and my mouth was filled with his seeds. I let that shit slide down my throat. I thought I was about to throw up. I'd never done that shit before. I saw some chick do it on a flick. I kept my composure though. I had to make this nigga think I knew what I was doing. He was in total awe.

"Damn, baby… I ain't know you could get down like that. Your sister would never do no shit like that!"

I shot him a wicked look and said, "Let's get something straight. If we gonna be fuckin' around don't keep throwing my sister's name up in my face. There's a lot of shit that I do that my sister ain't built to do and never will be able to do! So please don't compare me to her, because there is no other bitch that walks this earth that gets down like me!"

I strutted to the bathroom and slammed the door. I turned on the water and started bagging up. *I know that nigga is lost for words*, I thought. I stuck my finger down my throat and threw up. That was the nastiest shit I'd ever tasted in my life. It felt like I drank a glass of thick salt water. I knew I had to step my game up so I had to do whatever it took. I brushed my teeth and went back into the bedroom.

Rashawn was sprawled across the bed, dick dangling.

"Come on, baby, climb on top."

I looked at him as to say, *nigga please*. I switched across the room ass naked and grabbed my box of food.

"Is this mine?"

He was confused. "Yeah, but come on baby... give me some lovin'. I couldn't keep you off my mind while I was handling my business earlier," he whined.

"I bet. Looking at her is like looking at me," I said under my breath.

He was sitting on the bed looking like a sick puppy. "Damn, Lyse, why you being so mean? Just last night you were sweet as pie, now you on some other shit," he complained.

I opened up my food and began to eat. I propped one of my legs up on the chair so he could get a clear view of my girl. I watched him from the corner of my eye lusting over my body. I licked syrup that fell on my fingers slowly so he could take it all in. A few minutes later I noticed his hands moving underneath the sheets. *Nasty bastard*, I thought. He sat there and jerked off while I ate. I sat my food down and went to take a shower. Of course a few minutes later he joined me.

Later that afternoon he took me to the Baltimore Harbor. He'd spent so much cash it was ridiculous. I tried to act like I wasn't impressed, but I was jumping for joy on the inside. That's how things went over the next few weeks. It didn't take me long to find Rashawn's weakness. Like most men, he had a thing for "freak broads." I let him stick it in any and every hole, and he gave me what I wanted.

When he would act up I took it away, and just like a dog who wanted a bone he begged and would do whatever he had to do to please me. We would take on these little shopping ventures, get a room and fuck. Once I was sleep he would sneak out to satisfy Kat and come back like nothing ever happened. I think a few of his side bitches got a little vexed. I made sure I took up all of his free time and money.

Chapter 10
LET THE GAMES BEGIN

One day in late July we were leaving the movies. We went over the state line to West Chester so no one saw us together. We were walking hand in hand giggling and all that good stuff. All of a sudden he stopped in his tracks. He let go of my hand and started walking towards the concession line. I looked over in that direction and almost pissed myself. Kat was in line with that lame dude from her school. *Oh shit!* I thought. She didn't see me but Rashawn saw her, and if looks could kill she would be one dead bitch.

I hurried and grabbed him by his arm. "Baby, no, now is not the time!"

He pushed my arm away.

I grabbed him again. "Baby, no! Don't go over there. What if she sees me… you can't do this here!"

He stopped and listened to me.

"Baby, come on, let's go home. It's not worth it. Come on, baby. I know you're hurt… I know how much you love her. I'm hurt too, baby. How do you think I feel when I hear them fucking in the other room damn near every night I'm home? I feel bad because she is betraying you. I don't like to see those I truly love hurt." I laid it on thick.

That nigga looked like he was about to cry. He was heartbroken. I managed to pull him away from her view and we walked to his car. I drove his big boy Benz straight to his condo. I was glowing on the inside. This was my way in. He had never allowed me or any other female besides Kat to come to his place. I took the keys out the ignition.

"So, you want me to call a cab, or would you like me to keep you company?"

He got out of the car, came around to my side and opened the door. When he held my hand and led me to elevator I knew it was on and popping.

I admired his condo. Kat definitely didn't do the decorating; everything was in warm earth tones. There was an aquarium that was built into the wall and plush cream carpet that I was afraid to even step on with my shoes. The living room was so spacious, adorned in bronze and gold accessories. Beautiful African masks hung on the walls. I felt like I was in a cultural museum. Rashawn sat on the mahogany colored Italian leather couch and broke down. A waterfall of tears fell from his eyes. I couldn't believe what I was witnessing.

"I love that girl! I can't believe she's out in public with that mother fucker. Like its cool or some shit," he sobbed. He took the picture of Kat from his table and threw it across the room. "I'ma kill that bitch! All the shit I've done for her. I gave her my fucking life. I can have any bitch I want… Lyse, all types of bitches be throwing their pussy at me, I fuck some but that's it. They are just a fuck. I don't take care of them like I do Kat. I mean, shit… I don't do nearly half the shit I do for her, for you, and you treat me like a fucking king compared to her. I mean, you both have a shitty attitude at times, but I love that… I love her!"

I rocked in his lazy boy recliner watching his sickening performance. *So the truth comes out,* I thought. He threw shit all around the house. I went behind him picking up. The more he proclaimed his love for Kat, the more I felt used, and the rage in me grew. I stayed silent the whole time. God knows I had a lot to say. I waited until he was finished snapping. He sat on the couch and pulled me onto his lap.

"Lyse, you wouldn't do me like that, would you? You appreciate me don't you?"

I told him what he wanted to hear. "Baby, why don't you call her? Maybe it's innocent. If she has nothing to hide she'll tell you where she is at?"

I handed him his cordless phone and he did what I asked. I knew damn well it wasn't innocent. I just wanted him to feel like shit. Five minutes later the phone went flying through the air. I jumped off his lap in case he wanted to lash out at me.

"What, baby, what she say?"

He reached out for me and pulled me on the couch next to him. He buried his face in my breast, and I rubbed his head.

"She said she was out with Karen at a fucking poetry reading!"

I giggled silently, *Karen?* She should have known better then to say her name. Everybody knew Karen wouldn't be at no damn poetry reading, or anywhere else. Her man T.C. kept her ass on lock. She needed permission from him to piss.

I whispered in his ear, "You don't need her... you got me now. Let me help you get her off your mind."

I stood and undressed and did just that. I gave my body to Rashawn in every way imaginable. He was impressed at my talents for my age and the little experience I had. I guess I was a very talented at seventeen. It didn't take me long to get his mind off of Kat. Before I knew it, those tears were dried up, and he was calling my damn name. We fell asleep in each other's arms. I almost felt bad for him. I had to keep it in my mind that he was the enemy. I was just a substitute in his eyes.

The next morning I left before he had a chance to wake up. I caught the number fifteen bus to New Castle. That's where Kee had parked my truck. She was staying with her aunt, who now had custody of her children. A few weeks back when Kee had Little Boaz he was born strung out. She forgot to tell me that she had picked up a little habit of sniffing dope along with Bo. I knew Spinx and his boys dabbled in it from time to time. His excuse was it made his dick stay hard all night. Which was true, dope dick was awesome, but so not worth taking a risk of getting addicted. Anyway, the state got involved and put her kids in foster care until her Aunt took charge.

Mrs. Patterson, her aunt, was a sweet person. She was a little strict, church going and old fashioned. She took good care of the kids and made sure Kee went to all of her meetings. She'd even convinced Kee to enroll in GED classes so she could go away to school next year. I was happy for her. I thought she would be ok, as long as she stayed away from the Hills. I wanted to go in and say hi, but it was extremely too early. I got in my truck and headed home. I couldn't wait to see Kat. I knew she would tell me all about her night with the lame.

When I pulled up I noticed she wasn't alone. I pulled out my cell and called Rashawn. He picked up on the first ring.

"Baby, why you leave so early, I wanted to take you out to breakfast?" he whined.

I fixed my clothes and lied. "Oh, baby, I'm sorry. I have a lot to do today. I have an interview at the bank at 2 pm."

There was a brief pause.

"Interview… you trying to go to work, Lyse? You don't need to work… I can take care of you. I mean, it's good to see you trying to do something productive, but I thought you were going to school in the fall?" he asked, puzzled.

I could tell he was impressed but also shocked that I'd said something about getting a job. It was my plan to apply for one, but not just yet.

"You do take good care of me, baby, but I want my own place. I mean, you can't take care of her and me and be fair about it. Plus, I'm tired of coming to Kat's house and her little friend be running through the house *naked* and shit, playing little *love* games. Prime example, I can't even park in the garage or the driveway. His black Mustang is in the way. I know it's him because he has North Carolina tags," I complained.

I tried to act as if I was agitated. I just wanted to get under his skin. I could have cared less if she had ten niggas running around swinging from the ceiling. Rashawn had gotten quiet on me.

"Rashawn... Rashawn... you there?" I knew he was still on the phone I heard him breathing hard. He was mad. I laughed silently. "Look... I'm gonna call you back. I'm about to go in the house and I don't know where Kat is. I mean, they may be in the living room... who knows. I don't want you to hear anything that may upset you more. So remember, baby, you have my love now. I can help you get through this... if you want me too."

He spoke up, "Don't hang up; put me on speaker phone so I can hear what's going on. That's my fucking house!"

Oh my God, he is acting like a bitch. Speaker phone? I thought. "Baby, I don't think that's a good idea. What if you hear the wrong thing and have an outburst? They can hear you through the speaker and then she'll think I set her up."

He wasn't trying to hear that. "Lyse, just do it!"

I put the phone on speaker. I opened my purse and placed

it inside, in a position that would allow Rashawn to hear. Before I walked in the house I tested to make sure he could hear. When I went in the house Kat and her friend were sitting at the table eating breakfast. This chick had on what I guess was one his shirts and only had on boxers.

Kat got up from the table immediately. "Hey, I didn't expect you home this early," she said nervously.

I walked over to the table and sat down. "I bet you didn't." I smirked.

The shirt she had on was a little see-through, she had nothing on underneath.

"Yuck! Can you go put some clothes on? I don't want to see your tits and ass first thing in the morning!" I said loudly.

She laughed. "Shut up, hussy. I didn't expect you to be home. Allen and I just got up and he decided to cook me breakfast before he went to work." Kat was smiling from ear to ear. I hadn't seen her like that in a minute.

I turned my attention to Allen. "So, you're the guy that's been bangin' my sister's back out… you guys need to quiet down a bit, I need my beauty rest," I teased.

He smiled an uncomfortable smile.

"No need to be embarrassed, honey. Sounds like you really be putting it down, look at her, she's glowing like a bulb." I added.

He put a bunch of food in his mouth and looked at Kat as to say, *Shut her ass up*.

Kat was cheesing. "What are your plans for the day?" she tried to change the subject.

"I have an interview today at 2 pm," I said quickly. I had to stick to the lie because Rashawn was listening.

She almost spit her food out. "You, a job, yeah right, where?"

I rolled my eyes, this bitch wanted to know everything. I just said the first bank that came to my mind. "MBNA… it's for a Customer Service position."

She looked at Allen and he looked at me. He picked up his napkin and wiped his mouth.

"Oh, so you're going to our open house today? I'm a supervisor at the site next to the hospital. I'll be there conducting a few interviews," he said. "Do you have any customer service experience?"

Me and my mouth, I thought. I had no intention of going to any damn interview, now I was stuck. He talked my head off for the next twenty minutes about his company and how they had scholarships and all this other crap. I didn't get interested until he told me how much money I would make and about the incentives. I agreed to meet him at the interview. He told me he would make sure I was hired. Kat was sitting there beaming.

I excused myself and went to my room. I sat my purse down and noticed my phone was still on. I had forgotten all about Rashawn. I figured he had already hung up. I took the phone off of speaker and he was still there.

"Baby, you there?" I asked.

I could hear him whimpering. *This mother fucker is weak as hell,* I thought. His ass was crying again. I couldn't believe people actually feared him. He was starting to become a complete turn off, but I had to stay focused. The goal was to make this nigga think I loved him and make his ass love me, because as you know, love conquers all.

Chapter 11
PLAYING NYCE

"That feels so good. Girl, you keep spoiling me like this you gonna make me put a ring on that finger," he moaned.

Rashawn lay back on his lazy boy, and I was on my knees massaging his feet. He was in heaven. This was one of the special things I did to make him feel like a king.

I would clean his apartment in the nude every Sunday. He'd watch as I sashayed around the room, vacuuming and picking up behind him. He would be on the phone conducting business. I would bend in front of him so he could see a full view of my ass and girl from the back. His mouth would literally water. I wouldn't say a word the whole time, my body language spoke for me.

A whole month had passed since the movie encounter. Some things had changed. For one, I was now employed at MBNA. Allen stuck to his word. I started a week after my interview. At first I wasn't feeling the hours. They had me working Monday thru Thursday from noon until 9:00 pm. Sometimes they would try to stick some overtime on me and that meant twelve hour shifts. I complained until I saw my first check. I felt good about myself. I had finally earned my own money. I liked the fact that no one could hold anything over my head.

Rashawn wasn't feeling the job situation at all. He wanted me to depend on him for everything. The money he was giving me had doubled since I started working. I didn't even need to touch my checks. I just deposited them in my account. I even thought about getting my own place, but I soon changed my mind because I basically lived at the hotel or Rashawn's.

Speaking of Rashawn, he'd changed for the better. Well in my eyes he did. He had begun to despise Kat. Don't get me wrong, he still fucked with her, but you could see the change in his behavior around her. They usually took big trips like every other month. They hadn't been any where since Memorial Day. Matter of fact, he was taking me to the Bahamas for my birthday in a couple of weeks.

Kat went away to North Carolina with Allen to meet his family. They had been hot and heavy lately. I mean, Kat was even bringing this nigga lunch on his break. I didn't have to tell that one. Rashawn found out on his own when he dropped me off at work and saw the two cuddled up on a bench. He tried to play it off like it didn't affect him, but I know it was burning a hole through his heart. I knew he was about to do something dumb, so I called off the next day and took his mind off of it.

The phone rang. I was about to apply the lotion on his other foot, but he asked me to leave the room because it was business. I did as I was told. I washed my hands and checked on the roast I was cooking in the crock pot. My mom always said the way to a man's heart was through his stomach, so I paid close attention when she cooked. Kat, on the other hand, was too busy trying to be glamorous. I hadn't really spoken to my mom since the graduation. I turned the roast off.

I decided to take a ride to the Hills to go check on my mom. I wrote Rashawn a short note and handed it to him as I walked out the door. He showed me his approval by nodding. It wasn't like I needed his permission to go see my mom, but it built his ego when I asked to do things. Twenty minutes later I pulled up in front of my mom's house. There was a big U-Haul truck pulling away. My mom's Cavalier was parked in the driveway, loaded with boxes. I ran into the house to see what was up. My mom was in the kitchen stacking boxes in the middle of the floor.

"What are you doing?"

She looked very tired. She had her hair pulled back in a ponytail that hung towards her mid-back. She wore a white limited T-shirt that read U.S.A. and a pair of navy stretch pants. She looked cute to be in her mid-forties. She continued packing the box.

"What does it look like I'm doing? I'm moving out of this hell whole!" she snapped.

I sat my purse down and began helping her with the boxes. She snatched the box from my hand. "I don't need your help, Nalyse! You've helped enough."

I instantly caught an attitude. I had no idea what her issue was. She had been acting shitty with me since the graduation. I stepped back and gave her the evil eye. "What is your problem? I haven't done anything to you… you been acting funny with me since graduation. I try to call and you blow me off."

She stopped what she was doing and put her hands on her hips. She had a look of revulsion on her face. She closed her eyes and took a deep breath. "Why are you here? I sent all your belongings to Kat's earlier. There's nothing here for you. You can't come running to me when things get bad anymore. I am moving in with Dave. He proposed to me and I am moving on with my life. My job is done!"

She was angry and I had no idea why. She couldn't even look me in the face.

I grabbed my purse. I was becoming disgruntled and had to get out of there. "I just wanted to see how you were and tell you I have a job. I'm doing well for myself. But before I leave I have one question, when did I ever come to you when things were bad for me?" I hissed. I'd struck a nerve.

She became defensive and jumped up in my face. "I don't know who the hell you're talking to, Nalyse, I am your mother! You think you're so high and mighty and you have everything, but you ain't shit. I know what you're about, and I am ashamed to call you my daughter. Kat told me how you got pregnant by that Spinx character. He is a grown man, Nalyse, and I raised you better. She told me about the fights in school and how you had that girl cut up. I even know you were most likely the reason Rashawn was attacked at the graduation. Your animal friends did that. That boy cares about you. He looks at you like a sister. They should have never given you that truck. You don't deserve it. I heard how you were running around flashing money. Where did you get it? I know your so called job isn't paying you that much! Your drug dealer man gave it to you? Did he leave you a stash to hold him down? I should bring charges on his ass; he was raping you all those years. He ruined you!"

She was belligerent, yelling and cursing me out. I stood back in disbelief and watched her Emmy performance. Now I could see where Kat got it from. After a good twenty minutes she had tired herself out.

"Leave, I can't look at you, just leave!" she screamed. She started to cry and pushed me towards the door.

I was pissed. There was no way I was leaving. I sat there and listened to her rant and rave. Now it was my turn. "You gotta lot of nerve! Rashawn is a fucking drug dealer and you know that shit. So it's ok for Kat to get nice things? Oh yeah, I forgot it's cool for her, because Rashawn was bringing money in the house. He took care of you, too, so it was cool. As for the fights in school, you would have known if you weren't busy chasing Mr. Dave and living at your job. You were too busy trying to get your ass wet. You ain't have time for me. I was always here, you wasn't, so don't blame me for your fucked up parenting skills. And as for Kat, she ain't shit! Did you know she's fucking another nigga all up in Prince Rashawn's house? Hmmm… I bet you didn't know that, did you? So what you want, mom, you need me to drop you a few bills? If that's what you want I got it! And ain't no nigga give it to me. I got a job! A real one! I'm not wiping ass for $8.50 an hour." I folded my arms and smirked.

I knew that hurt her pride. Before I knew it, she hauled off and slapped me right across my face. It stung like hell, but I didn't let it faze me. I laughed at her as I walked to the door. She was behind me, looking like she wanted to fight. I couldn't hit my mom, so I got out of there quick. I ran through the front door. She ran outside the door ranting and raving. Everyone outside stopped what they were doing and watched. You wouldn't have thought I was her child the way she was carrying on. Her words were venomous. I was cool with it. *Jealousy is a mother fucker,* I thought. She stood at the bottom of her driveway screaming as I drove pass.

I waited until I was across the street before I rolled down my window and yelled, "By the way, how you accept a proposal from a married man? Dumb ass!"

She shut up with the quickness and hurried in the house.

I was vexed. I pulled up at Kat's and busted through the door. Before I could say a word she jumped on me. She was throwing punches towards my face. I started throwing them back. We tussled on the floor knocking shit over. I finally managed to get her off of me. I kicked her square in her mouth, and blood shot from her lip. She grabbed me by the hair and tried to fling me back on the floor. I got loose and ran to the kitchen and grabbed a knife.

"Ok, bitch, come on! I'll slice your fucking ass to pieces. Come on, bitch! You want to sneak people!" I shouted.

She backed away and wiped the blood from her mouth. Kat had a murderous look in her eyes "You disrespected my mom! You dirty bitch! How low is that, calling your own mother a bitch? I'ma kick your fucking teeth out. Put the knife down, you think you're so fucking grown! Your ass has no place to go, because as of today your ass is outta here. Get your shit and get the fuck out!" she ordered.

I laughed. "Bitch, I ain't got to stay in your piece of shit townhouse. I can get one two times bigger than this shit. I don't need you or mommy. Y'all ain't really do shit for me, but treat me like I don't measure up to y'all."

She laughed like she was insane. "Nobody said that. That's your fucked up mind thinking that. I guess you got a complex because you were second when it came to Spinx. You'll always be that side chick. You're too hood. It's all about you. You're selfish, don't no real nigga want a selfish brat by his side. You're just a little trophy piece, nothing to get serious with. That's why Brock didn't want you." She laughed.

I laughed with her sarcastically. I wanted so bad to tell her that someone actually did want me, someone like her so-called man. I wondered how she would feel if I told her how he licked my ass every night, but now was not the time. I put the knife down. She watched me as I walked out the door.

She followed me running her trap, "Where the fuck you

going? Get your shit and take a cab. That truck ain't leaving here!"

She ran behind me, trying to get to the truck. I jumped in before her and locked the doors. She was banging on my windows. I climbed to the back and pulled a Louisville Slugger from under the seat. She backed away when she saw it. I got out the car and went over to her Lexus and bashed out the back window.

"Side chick that, bitch!" I sneered.

She screamed like someone shot her ass. I jumped in my truck and pulled off. I was beyond hurt and angry. My cell phone rang.

"What, bitch?" I yelled.

A familiar voice said, "Whoa, I know it's been a minute but damn. What I do?"

I looked at the phone in shock. God must have heard my prayers. I was so relieved. I pulled over at the gas station and talked to my old friend. Two hours later I was on a flight to Atlanta.

Chapter 12
COMPLEX SITUATIONS

"Happy 1996 Philly!" shouted the DJ over the microphone. Everyone raised their bottles and glasses of champagne towards the sky. People were hugging each other. I spotted a few couples tonguing each other down. Rashawn and his boys were over at the picture booth posing in front of the big wall that had the words *"Gotham Night Club"* painted across it. I watched from the VIP section sipping on my virgin Pina Colada. I was tired, hungry and ready to go home.

I felt swift movements in my stomach that felt like butterflies. I looked down at my round little pouch and smiled. "I know… mommy's hungry too." I was four months pregnant. I'd found out shortly after our trip to the Bahamas.

When I told Rashawn he was ecstatic. I had mixed feelings about it. I wasn't ready to be a mother just yet, but it definitely made things better for me. Kat wasn't really an issue anymore. She would basically deal with Rashawn when money was low. I knew she suspected he was messing with someone else, but she just didn't know who. She didn't care because that gave her more time with "Lamo Allen." I knew when she found out about us she was going to flip, especially when she heard a baby was on the way. Rashawn told me not to worry about it. He said he would fix everything before the baby was born.

When I came back from the Bahamas I didn't have anywhere to live. Rashawn fixed that quick. He got me a luxury apartment out in Bear. School Bell Apartments were top of the line. I had a fireplace, washer and dryer, fitness center, spa, dishwasher, detached garage and so much more. You know he fully furnished it. I had pink leather furniture in the living room, a king-size brass four post bed and I had a bangin' Pioneer stereo system with a fifty-two inch TV. My place was laid. It was too hot for me not to show off.

So much had changed over the past few months. Before I went to Atlanta Rashawn's business had been dropping. His workers were getting locked up left and right. Of course I didn't know what was going on. He never talked to me about it. I wasn't schooled about everything until I arrived in Atlanta.

My "friend" told me all the problems Ra-Ra and his team were having. He also told me how we could use this to our advantage. My intention was to go down south to relax. Instead I was in boot camp for "the takeover." I was taking a crash course, "The Art of Hustling 101," and not just pushing drugs. There was more to it than that. In my own way I was already a hustler but now I had perfected the art.

The whole time I was away Rashawn blew up my phone. I heard nothing from Kat or my mom. I went back to Delaware a week later. I lied about my whereabouts. I told him I was in Dover with one of my girls from school. I also told him that I had been talking to an old friend of mine that happened to be a major player in the game. I lied and told him that I heard people talking about how he was losing his status in the city. He was offended and tried to act like everything was cool. I told him I knew a way to fix his problem.

I explained how I could introduce him to a "new" connect and a new way to get his product. He didn't take me serious at first, but when I told him it was Spinx's old connect that brightened his day. He knew that Spinx had some good shit. He was all ears for what I had to say. I told him that everything would have to go through me, but he didn't like that. I explained to him that the connect didn't know I was dealing with Rashawn. I said he thought that I was handling business for Spinx until he got home. I made it seem as if he wouldn't deal with Rashawn because he was loyal to Spinx. I even told him we could do a trial run so he could just test everything out. Of course his greedy ass fell for it.

The next day he gave me the money to make the transaction. No less than twenty-four hours later his package was being delivered by UPS to the abandoned house across the street from his Aunt's apartment. I'd left a note on the door of the house for the package to be left on the step. We watched from the window as he left the package and pulled off. I went on the porch and gave one of the junkies $10 to go get the package off the steps. Of course they did it gladly and handed me the box.

Once inside I opened the package. My eyes sparkled when I caught a glimpse of the snow white substance. I called Rashawn over, who was paranoid as hell, and showed him what lay beneath the Styrofoam and coffee grounds. He was astonished as well. Rashawn immediately called his workers. Before the day was over we had a few young girls at three different Western Unions. They were sending the maximum amount of cash they could send without using identification. They used fictitious names when doing the transactions. Within a months time Rashawn was on his way to becoming a future millionaire.

I'd let my girl Kee in on my secret affair with Rashawn. At first she wasn't with it. She thought I was really fucked up for messing with my sister's man, but after I schooled her on what my main goal was her thoughts quickly changed. Rashawn hadn't been so secretive about our affair either. After a few of his boys started to tell him how they saw Kat in public with Allen I guess he figured two could play that game. He started taking me to family functions, parties, and even on a few of his business ventures. I knew I was a pawn, but I didn't care. I already knew how the game was going to end.

••••••••••••••••••••••••••••••

"Ms. Nyse, would you like to know the sex of the baby?" Dr. Angler asked as she wiped the jelly from my stomach.

I had just finished my twenty-seventh week ultra sound. I looked up at Rashawn to see what he wanted to do. He eagerly shook his head yes. I told her we wanted to know, and she told us we were having a boy.

Rashawn practically jumped from his skin. He was overly excited. "Yeah, that's what I'm talking about!" he yelled as he rubbed my stomach and kissed me. "Thank you, baby, you just made me that happiest man in the world," his voice cracked.

He wrapped his arms around me tightly. I was a little taken back. I knew this nigga wasn't about to cry. Dr. Angler had a warm smile on her face. She quietly exited the room.

"Rashawn, baby, I want to get dressed now."

He broke his embrace. I climbed off the bed and began to dress. He watched me with teary eyes. I tried not to look his way. This was truly an emotional time for him, and I wasn't trying to catch feelings.

On our way out of the office she gave us a picture of the ultra sound. Rashawn took the one that said "it's a boy". He said he wanted to show it to his mother. I gave him a fake smile. I knew she would love that.

A few weeks ago he'd decided to come clean with his mother. He told her the truth about our relationship and that I was carrying his baby. She wasn't too thrilled about it. Matter of fact, she cursed him out badly and called me all types of conniving bitches. She even threatened to tell Kat about it. That's when I panicked. Rashawn was pissed. He took his mother upstairs to talk in private. An hour later she came down and apologized. I don't know what he said, but ever since she had been sweet as pie.

Rashawn rambled on about the baby all the way back to the apartment. He talked about all the fresh gear the baby would have and how he was gonna be a beast at basketball and football. He was planning his life out before he even took his first breath. I just nodded and agreed to what he was saying. Truth be told, my mind was far away from what he was saying.

A feeling of victory was coming over me. I'd finally had everyone where I wanted them. Kat's face wouldn't leave my mind. I couldn't wait to see her face when she found out that her soon to be nephew was Rashawn's son. I knew she was with Allen, but I also knew she still had love for Rashawn. I'd read the cards she'd sent him on holidays. I'd heard the phone conversations they would still have. If she hated him that much she wouldn't still meet him at the Radisson every Thursday and Sunday night. He didn't think I knew those things, but I knew everything. I knew his every move.

I was out of breath when we hit the front door. I couldn't wait until he opened the door. When I heard the lock click open I rushed past him and practically ran to the bathroom. A sudden urge to urinate came over me quickly. I thought I was about to piss myself. I almost fell trying to get my pants down and get on the toilet seat. The water just gushed out, and some of it managed to get on my clothes. *Shit. Now I gotta take a shower,* I thought. I just wanted to lie down and relax.

I reached over to the tub and ran the water. Once I was finish I gathered my pissy clothes and placed them in the hamper. I wrapped the towel around me and headed to my room. I heard Rashawn in the living room bragging to one of his boys about his new son. I shook my head. *He's so damn stupid. He better shut up about it before one of those jealous mutha fuckas put a bug in Kat's ear,* I thought. I lay across the bed in my towel and before I knew it I was drifting off to sleep.

•••••••••••••••••••••••••••••••

It had been a week since my doctors' visit, and Rashawn hadn't left my side. It was starting to get on my nerves. I couldn't even shit without him standing at the door talking about his soon to be son. The only time I had any peace or privacy was when he was sleep. I knew my "friend" had to be worried about me. I usually called him every day and he hadn't heard from me in over a week. I was determined to call him tonight. To make sure that would happen; I'd slipped a sleeping pill in Rashawn's tea to get him out of the way.

He was sitting on the couch watching GoodFellas, for the millionth time. I passed him his drink and cuddled up next to him. I watched as he gulped it down to my satisfaction. Not even a good twenty minutes later he was snoring. I turned off the TV, grabbed the phone and went on the balcony. It was cold as hell; I should have grabbed my mink. I dialed the number and damn near on the first ring he picked up.

"Baby, everything all right?" he asked.

I damn near had an orgasm at the sound of his voice.

"Yeah, it's cool, I'm sorry for not getting back to you sooner. I found out that I am having a boy and Rashawn went a little overboard with it. He acts like I'm about to have the baby any minute, he won't leave my side."

It felt funny talking about the baby with him. I remember when I found out I was knocked, I was afraid to tell him. I didn't want it to mess up our plans to be together after all this was done. I loved this man. Had things not went down the way they had I would have been with him in Atlanta and not here playing games with Rashawn.

I remember the night he called to let me know the plans for our house was finished. I'd busted out crying on the phone. He immediately got upset; he thought that nigga had put his hands on me. He was about to come up here, so I had no choice but to tell him the truth. I blurted out that I was pregnant and I was so sorry. He fell silent for a few minutes. I knew he was hurt, I heard it in his voice. He said it was ok, things like this happen all the time. He knew the game that we were playing, and he knew what the consequences could be. He told me he loved me and we would make this work. He said the baby was gonna need a father anyway once that nigga was gone. I managed to smile a little, too. But deep down inside I knew this shit was going to get out of control, and someone was going to get seriously hurt. I just prayed it wasn't me.

We talked for a couple of hours before I heard Rashawn moving in the living room. He must have felt the cold air from the patio doors. I told my friend I had to go and I loved him. He told me he loved me back and to be safe.

Before he hung up he said, "Nalyse, thank you for everything you're doing for us."

I held the phone to my ear. "I just hope I make it out alive," I whispered.

I dialed Kee's number and hung up like I always did, just in case Rashawn got the urge to hit redial to see who I'd called. He was slowly getting off the couch, holding his head. I tried to play concerned.

"You ok, baby?" I asked and rubbed his back.

He seemed a little dazed. I grabbed his hand and helped him to the bedroom. He fell onto the bed and was out again. I rolled my eyes. I had to remind myself this was only for a little while longer.

The next morning I woke up to an empty bed. I smiled in relief. I had gotten used to waking up with his dick in me. I looked at the clock and it was a little after noon. *Damn, I must have really needed that sleep*, I thought. I rolled out the bed and went to the bathroom to freshen up. I peeked in the living room and it was empty. *Great! I got the place to myself*, I thought. I decided that I wasn't going anywhere today. I was going to sit around and talk to my baby. I really needed to check on things around the way, but I could just call Kee to get an update.

I went into the kitchen to take my vitamin and make some raisin toast. I didn't even have a chance to get the bread out the bag before the phone rang. *I know it ain't this nigga*, I thought. I looked the caller I.D., and it was Kee calling from Caree's house. I noticed that it had the number six next to the name. I wondered why she had called here that many times and why I hadn't heard the phone ringing.

"Hello?" I answered annoyed.

"Bitch, why ain't you been answering the fucking phone!" she yelled.

"Hold up, who you calling a bitch? And what's wrong with you calling my house yelling and shit!"

"We got a serious issue. Two of our packages were stolen this morning, and I think I know who did it…"

My heart dropped. "Do you know how much fuckin' money that is? How did that shit happen? Who did it? Did you call your squad? They need to handle this, ASAP!" I questioned her thoroughly. I began to pace the floor. That was over $200,000 worth of shit that I'd stole from Rashawn. I felt my stomach knot up. I had to take a seat.

"Nyse, I called my peoples, but they're not going to budge… you see, my peoples were once his peoples, so they ain't my peoples no more. They back with him," she explained.

Why is she talking in riddles? I wondered. This was not the time for that. "Kee, who is he? What the fuck are you talking about? I ain't got time to play fucking *Jeopardy*." I was aggravated.

Kee whispered, "Spinx, he's out. I don't know how, but that nigga is out, and he knows what the fuck we been doing. He was sitting outside this morning when I went to one of the houses to pick up our shit. At first I didn't pay him any attention, but when I got closer he stepped out of this black Blazer. I almost pissed myself; it was like seeing a fucking ghost."

My body began to tremble. I was not ready for this shit. *How did he get out? I thought he was gone for sure,* I thought. I needed to call Rashawn, but I couldn't call him. He didn't know I'd set shit up in the Hills. I had to call my friend; he would know what to do.

"Kee, did he say anything to you?"

"Girl, that's the scary shit. He ain't say nothing, he just smiled at me. You know that smile he gives before Fatal comes and snatches your ass up. Look, as soon as I can, me and my kids are getting the fuck out of dodge, and I suggest you do the same. I love you, girl. Take the money you got and bounce!" she hung up.

I couldn't believe it. That bitch was going to bail on me after all I had done for her. My stomach began to cramp worse. I needed to call my friend and let him know that shit was fucked up. Before I got a chance to call the doorbell rang. I was scared to death. *What if this bastard found out where I live?* I thought.

I wasn't taking any chances. I went to the closet and pulled out Rashawn's .9 millimeter. I'd be damned if this nigga was gonna get me first. I made my way to the door and a sharp pain rang through my pelvis. I doubled over holding my stomach. The pain was so severe it bought tears to my eyes. The doorbell rang again. I took a deep breath and stood back up. I put the gun in the inside pocket of my robe and answered the door.

Chapter 13
SISTER SISTER

-Kat

A few days ago Allen and I were in a heated session when we were rudely interrupted by a knock at the door. At first I was going to ignore it, but the knocks became louder and more forceful. It got to the point where I thought they were going to bust the damn door down. I slowly slid off of Allen's love tool and wrapped up in a sheet. I went over to my window to see who it was. I noticed a supped up black Blazer out front and immediately panicked. I thought it was Rashawn in one of his boy's trucks.

I ran over to Allen and told him to hurry up and run in the spare room and to lock the door. I told him it was my boyfriend. At first he tried to be hard and was like, he's not going anywhere; he's tired of hiding our relationship. Allen was talking reckless. He didn't know my boyfriend's status. I'd never told him that I was involved with a notorious drug dealer. I just told him he was a very important man who could make people vanish. Allen lay in bed not budging. I begged and pleaded with him but he wouldn't move. Finally, I just said forget it. I took a deep breath and walked out the room.

I stopped at the bathroom and grabbed a towel, then wrapped it around my sweaty, naked, body. I would just tell him I was finishing my workout and about to hop in the shower. I said a short prayer before opening the door. When I opened it I couldn't believe who stood before me. Spinx black ass was grinning from ear to ear. I told him Nalyse didn't stay here anymore and was about to slam the door on him.

He pushed himself in the door, "Yo, wait a minute! I got to talk to you for a minute. Your sister is in a lot of trouble!" he barked.

That got my attention. I was mad at her and hadn't heard from her in months but I still cared about her. "What you mean she's in trouble?" I questioned.

He opened the door and walked past me. He looked me up and down before sitting on the couch.

"What… what are you looking at?" I snapped.

"Damn, girl, you are thick as hell," he said.

He acted like he wanted to touch my ass. I backed away from him and gave him a look. He knew I wasn't playing with his ass. He asked me to sit down because I was making him nervous. I ignored his request and kept standing.

He looked at me and grunted. "Yo, you ain't gonna like what I'm about to tell you. Your sister done set up shop and is moving crazy weight. She better be careful 'cause she's making a lot of enemies and I'm one of them. I heard that little bitch done turned the nigga she workin' for on to my connect, and they took over my spot." He was vexed.

I laughed to myself. Why would I care about that? I was confused to what the issue was. "Ok, so she's doing well for herself, she found herself a balla. Good for her, I guess. Is that all? I think Nyse can handle herself; I have nothing to do with that. And she won't listen to me anyway." I was about to show Spinx the door, but the next words from his mouth cut deep.

He sat back on my couch. "So, how do you feel about becoming a stepmom, or should I say auntie?" he said slyly.

I turned to him in disbelief. I couldn't have heard him correctly.

He added. "Oh, you didn't know… damn, my bad. You mean to tell me you didn't know your nigga was fucking your little sister? That's crazy." He chuckled and shook his head.

I didn't believe him. He wanted to try and hurt me. That was a lie. There was no way Rashawn would mess with Nalyse, or vice versa. Nalyse was wild and couldn't be tamed. She was loud and full of drama. Rashawn couldn't stand that type of chicks. My heart was beating a mile a minute. I couldn't catch my breath. I began to yell and scream for him to get out.

Allen must have heard all the commotion. He came running down the stairs to my aid. Spinx stood up when he saw him. Allen came behind me and put his arms around me. He asked me if I was ok and fixed his eyes on Spinx. Spinx laughed at the site of us together. He walked pass me and dropped a piece of paper with his number on it on the table.

"Now I see why you were blinded. Call me when you're ready to see the truth."

And just like that he was gone. Allen sat me on the couch and held me in his arms. He knew I was upset but didn't know why. He didn't ask either. He just held me as I cried in his arms.

Later that evening when Allen was asleep I called Rashawn. He didn't answer. I decided to go pay him a visit.

I arrived at his apartment and he didn't answer. I decided to use my key and noticed the locks had been changed. I knew I hadn't been coming up there for a minute, but damn, why change the locks? I decided to ride to his mother's; she would tell me what was up. When I got there she turned pale when she saw me. She seemed a little hesitant to let me in, but she did.

I walked pass her and took a seat at her dining room table. Her townhouse was really small. Everything in it was old fashioned but tasteful. I never understood why she didn't redecorate. It wasn't like her son didn't have the money to do it.

"Mom Liz, I can't seem to get a hold of Rashawn, do you know where he is?"

She stood in front of the door with her arms folded and lips tight. "Why don't you know where he is, isn't that your job, to know your fiancé's whereabouts?"

She was being very sarcastic and I didn't understand why. She was really distant and nasty. I decided to end my visit early. I started to hug her and she moved away. I was hurt. This woman had been like a second mother to me for years. I turned away to walk out the door. Before I was out I felt a tap on the shoulder. Ms. Gibbs was close to tears.

She gave me a big hug and whispered, "I love you, Katty, remember that."

Something wasn't right. She wanted to tell me something, I could tell. I told her I loved her and walked to my car. I sat there for a minute then picked up my cell phone. I pulled the paper from my pocket and dialed the number. Spinx answered the phone.

"I want some proof," I told him.

"Meet me School Bell Apartments right now," he replied.

"Now do you believe me, Katty? That little bitch is playing both of us. She's playing house with that nigga and carrying his baby. I should go merk both of these slimy mufuckas right now!" Spinx grunted. He took a long pull of his blunt before passing it.

I usually didn't smoke, but after the shit I'd just witnessed I needed something to ease the pain. I knew Nalyse had some shit with her, but I never thought she would go as far as getting pregnant by Rashawn. How could I have been so stupid? Why didn't I see it coming? But how could I? I hadn't seen or heard from her since the fight. *And Rashawn, oh my God, why would he do this to me? He would never deliberately hurt me like this... unless. Oh God, he knows... that little bitch must have told him about Allen,* I thought. I took another drag of the blunt and began to choke.

"Damn, Katty, you aight, baby?" Spinx asked. He passed me a Very Fine juice.

I drank it and tried to catch my breath. I coughed and said, "I'm cool. Whew... oh my God, what's in this weed?"

He gave me a devilish grin. "Baby, this that Wet, I heard about this shit in the joint. It will keep you high for a minute and keep your dick hard." He winked at me and licked his lips. "You might as well let me hit that. We can just flip that shit on 'em, ya know." He was grinning like the Grinch that stole Christmas.

I rolled my eyes. It would be a cold day in hell before I would let his black ass lay a finger on me. Hell, it was his fault that my sister turned into the cold hearted snake she was.

••••••••••••••••••••••••••••••••••••

As I approached the apartment door I prayed I would

catch them in the act. That would make it easier to blow his fuckin' head off. If we were in Maryland it would be considered a crime of passion and I would probably get off. I wouldn't be so lucky here, but who knows, the police would look at it as if I did them a favor.

I didn't know what was taking her ass so long to answer the door. She probably was in there fucking my man. I was getting disgusted by the minute. Nasty bitch! I couldn't believe she'd done this to me. I was her fucking blood. I knew I didn't treat her that bad; to do some shit like this. No words could describe how I felt about Rashawn. We were still seeing each other a few times a week. Just the thought of him making love to me and then going home and playing house with my little sister made me nauseas.

I pulled my little .22 out of my pocketbook and placed it in my jacket pocket. Just in case that mother fucker wanted to get stupid. I heard someone jingling the door. *Ok, Kat, take a deep breath, relax. I gotta make sure this goes smooth,* I thought.

The door opened and my heart broke into a thousand pieces at the site of Nalyse standing there with her big belly caring my fiancé's baby. I had to fight back tears. This was the ultimate betrayal. She stood there looking at me, eyes all big. I could tell she was surprised to see me. She was white as a damn ghost. The tension between us was so thick that you could cut it with a knife.

She stood there holding her stomach. She looked like she was in pain or something. I brushed pass her and went into the apartment. It was breathtaking. Her home was adorned with plush pink carpet, a salmon pink leather sectional, and a big screen TV. Everything was top of the line; I was amazed. Rashawn was holding out on me. Her place looked like it should have been in a fashion magazine.

"Wow, Lyse, you are doing incredibly well for yourself. I see you done got big time on me. Look at this place, it's beautiful, and look at you. Why didn't you tell me I was going to be an auntie? I know mommy would want to know she is going to be a grandma."

She stood there trembling. *Humph, no need to be scared now,* I thought. I sat down on her couch and patted for her sit next to me. She didn't move or say a word. I kicked my feet up on her glass coffee table. *That should get her hot,* I thought. Still no reaction, she stood there looking like a zombie. I was getting tired of the silent treatment. I decided to get straight to the point.

"Who's the father of your baby?" I inquired.

Just like that she snapped out of her trance. She moved slowly to the recliner and sat down. She folded her hands on her lap and that's when I noticed something red running down her legs. I looked over to the spot where she was standing and there was a puddle of blood. I immediately ran to her.

"Oh my God, Lyse, you're bleeding! Oh God, how far are you?" I was frantic.

Tears ran from her eyes; she acted like she was going to lose consciousness. I had to do something quick or she would lose the baby, or even her life. I picked up her phone and dialed 9-1-1. I looked at her, and for a brief moment something dark and wicked came over me. *I should just let her bleed out. That would make everything so much easier,* I shook the thought. I couldn't do that to my sister no matter how dirty she'd done me. I couldn't live with knowing I'd played part in her child, my niece or nephew's death.

Five minutes later the paramedics were in the apartment working on her. They said that she was in shock and going into premature labor. They asked me how far she was. I told them I had no idea, and I'd just found out she was pregnant.

He looked at me funny. I explained to him that we didn't talk often. I guess he was still confused on how I didn't know my own sister was pregnant. He asked if I was going to ride in the ambulance with her. I told him I would follow behind them.

When I got in the car I picked up the phone and called Rashawn. I didn't want him to know I knew the truth. Not yet, not until I knew if this baby was going to make it or not. He didn't pick up the phone. I left him a message telling him that something bad had happened and I needed him to come to the Christiana Hospital immediately.

I had to sit outside in the waiting room. The doctors were in there working on Nalyse. It had been over forty-five minutes and no one had been out to tell me anything. I thought about calling my mom. She had been worried sick about her the last few months. She was too stubborn to try to find out where she was. She dropped hints for me to do it.

After the fight we had Nalyse basically dropped off the face of this earth. I mean, everybody saw her but us. It's just funny nobody mentioned to me that she was sleeping with my man and having his baby.

I picked up the phone to call Spinx. I knew he would want to know what was up. Just as I started to dial the number I heard a frantic voice demanding to know where his wifey was located. *Wifey?* I wondered if he was talking about me or my sister. Rashawn and a few of his boys were giving the staff a hard time. The poor little fragile nurse looked like she wanted to haul ass. I decided to step-in before she had a damn heart attack.

"Baby, I'm over here!" I yelled, running towards him.

The look on his face was priceless. He looked like he was about to shit himself. His friends looked real dumb in the face, too.

"I see you got my message," I said hugging him.

He cocked his head to the side like he was confused.

"Rashawn, the message… about meeting me here…."

He looked like he didn't have a clue. He rubbed his hand over his head. "Yeah, I got it… what's up… why… why are you here? You all right?" he asked as he opened his arms for me to embrace him.

I wrapped my arms around his waist and looked him in the eyes. "How did you know to come to the Maternity section?"

There was that look again. Just as I was about to question him some more the doctors came out of the room. He was saved.

"Is there a Katina Nyse out here?" the doctor inquired.

I let go of Rashawn and went over to the doctor. I could tell he wanted come, but was too scared. I asked the doctor if everything was ok with my sister. He didn't tell me anything except that she wanted to speak with me.

-Nalyse

How in the hell did she find out where I lived? I thought. This was all too much for me. Spinx was out and Kat knew what was up with me and Rashawn. She tried to act like she didn't, but I know she did. I could see it all in her face. Especially when she saw my stomach, she wanted to bawl right there. She was just trying to play hard. My question is how did she found out?

My mind was racing. *I bet it was that bitch Kee. She was the only one close to me that knew what was up. This was probably all a set up. That's why she was leaving. I bet she split that pack with Spinx, told Kat what was up, then bounced*, I thought. I felt my pressure going up. *Chill, Nyse. I got to stay calm before this baby tries to come again,* I thought. Damn, this was not supposed to be how it ended. I had to come up with something quick. I knew Kat was gonna try to get back with Rashawn now. She'd blame all this shit on me. Then it came to me, I was gonna have to flip this shit.

I told Dr. Allen to have my sister come in after they were finished working on me. I explained that I wanted to tell her myself about my condition. He agreed and left out. I had to lay on my left side in silence. My pressure was up and I'd begun to dilate and go into labor. The doctor told me I had to be on complete bed rest in the hospital until it was time to deliver. In a way I was relieved, I wouldn't have to face the outside world for at least another month. I rested for a few moments until I heard the door open. Kat hurried to my bedside and started stroking my hair. I knew she was pissed, but her eyes had compassion.

"I'm sorry, Kat." I cried softly. "I didn't mean to do this… I really didn't… I wanted to tell you when it first happened but I knew you wouldn't believe me."

A puzzled look came on her face. She pulled a chair next to my bed and handed me a tissue. "What are you talking about, Nalyse? What wouldn't I believe?"

I wiped my nose and sobbed a little more. "I wanted to tell you… I know how much you love him, and I know y'all been together forever. I just… I just didn't think he would react that way… I didn't know he would do this to me… I thought he looked at me like a sister… I didn't know. Oh my God… I am so sorry!"

I hid my face with my hands. I peeked through the crack of my fingers and I could see her face turning red. I bet her heart was beating a mile a minute. She grabbed my hands and gently pulled them from my face.

"What… what did he do to you?" asked Kat. Her voice was cracking.

I tried to hide my smile. I had her right where I wanted her. I sat up in bed and took a deep breath. "One night I was at the mall. I saw Rashawn sitting on the bench with a vexed look on his face. I went over to him to say what's up. When he saw me he looked like he was about to breakdown. I sat next to him and asked him what was wrong. He told me he saw you and some other nigga hand in hand at the movies. I didn't know what to say after that. He told me he was about to go to the crib and turn it out."

Kat put her head down in shame.

"So, I told him I didn't think that was something he should do. Maybe he was just a friend or something, I'd tried to rationalize. He wasn't buying it, so I asked him to go to Bankshots to play pool for a while. After about a half hour of convincing he decided to go. I left my truck at the mall and got in his car. We hung out and we both had a few drinks. On our way back to the mall he told me he needed to get something from his crib. Of course I didn't see anything wrong with it, so I went in with him. Once inside we had more drinks and smoked a blunt or two. Before I knew it I had dozed off on his couch. Next thing I know I felt him unbuttoning my pants and putting his mouth all over me. I tried to stop him, but he was too strong."

Kat jumped from her seat. She was crying. "No… not Rashawn no… Nalyse, please, please, tell me you're lying, please tell me this is some sick joke," she pleaded.

I shook my head. "I'm so sorry; I can't tell you that… it's true. He raped me! Rashawn raped me and told me that he would get Fatal to handle you and ol' boy if I said anything. That's why I stayed away. That is, until I found out I was pregnant. That's when he put me in my own place. He doesn't live there. He just comes over and takes what he wants from me and leave. He thinks he owns me because I am carrying his child," I whimpered.

That was too much for her to handle. Kat dropped to her knees and let out a blood curdling cry. She was internally wounded. I knew I was wrong for the lie I'd just told. I had no choice. I didn't think about what the consequences would be when my family found out I had been playing house with Rashawn. My mother would really hate me, and my brother, Stack would never let me live this down.

-*Kat*

This can't be true. Rashawn… rape? My brain was ready to explode. I tried to think back to see if I missed any clues of him being capable of such an act. I came up with nothing. I sat back in the chair and took a deep breath. I glanced over at Nalyse and she was knocked out. I guess the meds had finally taken affect, she looked so peaceful. I wished I could feel what she was feeling, because at that moment I needed something to calm me down.

I picked up the phone to call my mother. Lyse had asked me to fill her in on everything. Well not everything… she wanted to leave out the part that she was carrying Rashawn's baby. I was kind of relieved, because I really didn't want to get into it with my mother. She would swear it was my fault for not reaching out to Lyse sooner.

Rashawn wasn't to know that I knew the truth either. Now that was going to be hard. I wanted him to pay for what he had done to us. I felt bad that he'd caught me with Allen, but he had been doing it to me for years. He just was good at hiding it. Besides, he really crossed the line raping my sister, then getting her pregnant and expecting her to keep it. Hell no! I would play this game of unawareness for a moment. But I swore on my life, he was going to pay one way or the other.

Not even fifteen minutes after I spoke to my mother she was busting through the door. She wasn't alone. Rashawn had managed to sneak in with her. He came over and started hugging all over me, asking if I was ok and was the boy ok. That was a dead giveaway right there. How did he know it was a boy? I didn't even know she was having a boy. I was so disgusted, but I played along. I explained to both of them what was going on. I told them she had gone in pre-mature labor, and they were keeping her in the hospital on bed rest and giving her steroids to strengthen the baby's lungs. Again his actions told on him, his ass had the nerve to go over and rub her belly.

This time my mom had a crazy look on her face and of course she asked him what he was doing. He was startled. He told her he was praying for his "nephew" and lil' sister to get well. She fell for it. I had to laugh. *Nephew, didn't he mean son?* I thought. I rolled my eyes. My mom gave him a big hug and told him she loved him.

Humph, she wouldn't be saying that if she knew he raped her daughter, I thought.

My mom sat on the edge of Lyse's bed and rubbed her hands. "Do you know who the father is?" she asked me.

Rashawn's eyes practically bulged out of his head. He stood up and went over to the window.

"A guy named Kevin. Kevin Brockman... he is really sweet, mommy. He is good for her."

Rashawn spoke up, "Kev... yo, that nigga is dead! Remember the explosion, he was burned alive. . If it was his she would have been had that baby!" he said sounding upset.

My mother said, "Oh my God, is that the young man they

are looking for? I thought they didn't find his body… I didn't know he actually died. But he can't be dead, because Lyse says he's the father. I know my baby ain't crazy. I liked that young man; he would be good for her." She added.

All the motherly love Rashawn had for my mom had just flew out the door. He looked as if he could have kicked her in her throat. I had to admit I was enjoying this.

"Well, mom, he is nice. And, Rashawn, he didn't die. They just assumed that it was him in the truck. Matter of fact, he put her up in a nice condo, sends her money, and is on his way up here to witness the birth of his baby." I rubbed it in.

Tears filled his eyes. He was hurt. He flashed a dirty look in Lyse's direction and bit his bottom lip. I knew he was truly pissed when he bit that lip. That was the look he gave before he was about to lose control. He knew he had no choice but to suck it up and let another man take credit for the things he did, or come out with the truth. I guess he chose to go along with the lie. He excused himself and stormed out the door.

My mom gave me confused look. "What was all that about?"

I shrugged my shoulders and told her that I was going after him to find out. I went out into the lobby and Rashawn was nowhere to be found. It was like he disappeared, but that was just fine. I really didn't want to talk to him right then anyway. There was someone else that I needed to chat with. I had a funny feeling something FATAL was about to happen to Rashawn.

Chapter 14
DESPERATE TIMES DESPERATE MEASURES

-Nalyse

"Hey, mommy," my voice slurred from all the medication they were feeding me through the I.V.

She stroked my face with tears in her eyes. This was the first time I had seen her since our little argument. I had to admit, I was glad that she was here with me. I just prayed that Kat kept up her end of the deal. I made her promise to act like this baby was Kevin's. She didn't think it would work because everyone thought he was dead. I didn't want to, but I had no choice but to tell her what was really up.

See, Kevin was far from being dead. The night his truck was ambushed he wasn't really in it. The body that was found in the truck was so badly burned that they couldn't be clear on who it actually was. They assumed it was Kevin, but it was actually Spade's body that was found. Spade was unaware that his house had been raided. He didn't know his brother blamed Kevin for the raid and was planning to have him killed. Spade was secretly seeing a chick from the city and didn't want his brother to know. Kevin was the only one who knew about it, so it wasn't unusual for Spade to call him for a ride home when he needed it.

Kevin suspected Spinx might have blamed him for what was going on. He'd decided to pick up Spade just for a little insurance, in case things got out of hand. Sadly for Spade, Kevin was right. Soon as Kevin's truck was spotted in the Hill's all hell broke loose. Shots broke out coming from every direction. Spade caught one in the temple almost immediately. Kevin managed to escape out the passenger side door before the cocktail bombs landed and the explosion occurred. He ran through the woods for safety and met up with Fae in the next development that connected with the Hills. He knew things might go sour so he had her on standby. They drove to Atlanta, where he already had a few things going for him. His plan was to come back up here and scoop me up when things cooled down, but he heard that I was messing with Rashawn, so he backed off. However, he couldn't get me off his mind. That's when he made the phone call to reach out to me and tell me how he really felt.

During that time I had just finished having the huge fight with Kat and my mom so I took him up on his offer to get away. Once I was down there I told him my true feelings for him. I explained that Rashawn was just a nigga I was trying to get what I could get from. That's when we came up with the plan to take over all of his spots. Kevin knew that Rashawn was weak for pussy so we used it against him. We didn't know I was already carrying the enemy's seed. Once I found out, Kevin was a little disappointed. He quickly got over it and vowed that when Rashawn was out of the picture he would step up as the baby's father and raise it as his.

When I told Kat he was living down south and was in perfect health she was shocked. She asked me if I was sure that Rashawn was the father. I told her there was no way possible it could be anyone else because I hadn't slept with anyone besides him. I explained that Kevin and I had never slept together. I guess that's why I loved him so much. He actually loved me for who I was, not for what's between my legs. To prove it to her I called him while she was there. I explained to him in our code what had happened. He told me he would be up on the next flight.

I knew she was overwhelmed with information. The poor chick didn't know if she was coming or going. I finally convinced her to go along with the story. Her only argument was what if Rashawn came clean. I wasn't worried about that, because he and I both knew damn well that wasn't going to happen. I told her to do me one favor, and keep him occupied. I didn't want him questioning me about Kevin or anything else for that matter.

"I missed you so much, mommy." I was lying on my left side holding my mothers hand.

"I miss you too, baby. I'm so sorry for the things I said to you that day. I was just hurt because you kept so much away from me. I'm your mother; you can talk to me about anything." She ran my hand over her cheek.

"I'm sorry, too. I should have never disrespected you the way I did. I had a lot going on, and I don't know… I guess I snapped."

"I know… I know, but that's the past and we'll keep that in the past. We have to focus on that baby of yours and make sure everything is fine with him. I have some good news. Nelson will be released in two months. They are giving him house arrest for six months and then he'll be done." She was really excited about that. I tried to be optimistic. But she and I both knew Stack was hard headed as hell and would end up right back in jail.

Dr. Allen entered the room. "Unfortunately, you are still contracting and dilating. How soon before the father will be here, because I doubt if you will make it through the night without going into full labor."

The baby wasn't trying to wait. I was so doped up I didn't even feel the contractions. Tears streamed down my face as he gave me the news.

"He's on his way," I informed him.

"Don't worry. Due to all of the new technology preemies now have a better chance of survival. I want to do an ultrasound to see where the baby is located. We are also going to take measurements to see what we are going to be dealing with during your labor," Dr. Allen informed us.

"Can I stay while you do what you have to do?" my mom asked.

"It's up to Ms. Nyse," said Dr. Allen.

"It's ok," I said.

They started the procedures and when everything was done the doctor told me that the baby was about two pounds and in position for delivery. He also said I had dilated to six centimeters. I guess that wasn't good, because my mother was crying uncontrollably. The nurse escorted her out of the room. They didn't want me to get upset because my blood pressure would go up more, and that wouldn't be good for me or the baby.

All of this was happening too fast. Kat finding out the truth, Kevin coming back to Delaware, Spinx being home, and now the baby was coming. I was scared to think what could happen next. I guess thinking it was enough, because no sooner than the thought left my head Rashawn came busting through the doors.

He was pissed, hurt, confused and concerned all at the same time. I could tell he had a lot to say and it wasn't going to be good, but now wasn't the time. Dr. Allen had the floor. He paused at the site of Rashawn, but I told him to continue. He informed us that he was going to give me a c-section; they didn't want to put too much stress on the baby. A vaginal birth would be very difficult due to our current health situation.

The baby would be going to the Neonatal Unit (NICU), and would most likely remain there until his original due date. Rashawn began to ask Dr. Allen questions about the likely hood of survival. Of course he couldn't give us a definite answer that he would survive. He just said what he was trained to say.

Before the doctor left out, he told me that the anesthesiologist would be in to prep me for surgery. Also, whoever was going in with me had to be ready when he came back. Before Rashawn could say anything I cut him off.

"Look, baby. I had to say something to get the heat off of us. I had no choice but to say Kevin was the father," I clarified.

He didn't say anything. He just leaned back in the chair with his hands behind his head and started taking slow deep breaths. I reached for his hand but he quickly snatched it away when my mother came in.

"Hi, mommy, are you feeling better?"

Her face was stained with dried up tears. She sat on the bed and gave me a big hug and held me tightly. "I love you so much, and I promise to be a better mother and grandmother." She kissed my cheek and turned to Rashawn. "Sweetheart, what are you doing here? Where's Kat?" she asked.

"I just wanted to come check on my little sis… you know… and Kat, I don't know where she's at… I haven't seen her since I left here earlier," he said. "Besides, I know the *father* ain't nowhere around, and I plan to be there for my *nephew*," he said with sarcasm, stressing the nephew.

I rolled my eyes and looked out the window. Little did he know the *father* would be in the picture, to bad he wouldn't. My mom gave him a hug and praised him for being such a good son-in-law. She went on to say she couldn't wait until he and Kat made it official and had children of their own. He laughed and agreed half heartedly. I guess he knew that whole little family thing was never gonna happen for them, especially not now.

We chit chatted for a few more minutes before the doctors and nurses came in to get me ready for surgery. I almost fainted at the sight of that huge needle that was going in my spine. I cried and held on to my mom as they inserted the needle in my back. Rashawn held my hand and told me to squeeze if I felt pain. To my surprise it was only a little pinch. I lay back and it felt like hot lava was running down my legs.

I kept saying. "Oh my God, my insides are burning."

They told me that was normal and it would soon go away. When it was time to roll me into the operating room the doctor asked Rashawn if he was ready to witness his child being born. He froze instantly. My mom spoke up. She informed the doctor that he was the uncle and she was going in with me. I knew that didn't sit well with Rashawn. He looked like a sick puppy. He gave my mom his camcorder and told her to film it for me. She was happy that he had it on him because she didn't have hers. It didn't even cross her mind to question why he had one at that time in the first place. She was just excited that she was going to be able to see her grandson being born. My mother went with the nurse so she could get scrubbed up.

Rashawn bent over and whispered in my ear, "You are not off the hook. You got a lot of explaining to do. Be strong in there for our son… I love you." He kissed me on the lips.

I smiled and closed my eyes.

-Kat

I called Lyse's hospital room, but there was no answer. I prayed everything was ok. I decided to call the nurse's station to see what was up. They let the phone ring forever. When the phone was finally answered the person seemed to have an attitude. I had to check her real quick. She apologized and told me that my sister was in delivery. I hung up the phone immediately. I picked it back up and called Rashawn. His answering machine picked up on the first ring. *Damn. He must be at the hospital with her,* I thought.

A jealous rage came over me. I wanted so bad to jump in my car and go to the hospital so I could bash his head in. Instead I just made myself an Apple Martini and patiently waited for my guest to arrive. I couldn't believe it had come to this. I grimaced at the thought of him fucking my sister. *If only them Chester niggas had came through at the graduation,* I thought. *None of this would be happening*. Just thinking about their screw-up pissed me off. I had paid them boys $3,000 apiece to end his life. I wanted to be free. God only knows how many times he'd threatened to kill me if I ever left him.

I wanted Nalyse to be free from Spinx too. I had everything set up perfectly. Once Rashawn was gone his boys would have automatically thought it was Spinx and his crew who set him up. Of course they would retaliate and kill Spinx. Unfortunately it didn't happen. I guess that's what I got for having amateurs do a professionals job. It wasn't that I didn't love Rashawn, I loved him too much. That's why he had to go. I would never be able to live life the way I wanted with him around. This time there would be no room for any sloppiness. I knew just the right person who would be able to make this happen.

I finished my drink and looked at the time. It was 9:30 pm. She was late. I picked up the phone and called her cell. She told me she was just around the corner. When I hung up the phone rang. I picked it up.

"Hello?" I heard an excited voice on the other line. It was Rashawn.

"Hey, baby! Umm, why ain't you here supporting your mom and sister?" he asked.

I couldn't believe he had the nerve to call me from the damn hospital.

"I was coming in the morning. My mom is there and I thought Brock was supposed to be on his way up there too… but why are you there?

He fell silent for a minute. "I was looking for you. I know this is a stressful time, so I wanted to be here with my family," he said sincerely.

I guess he was really going to play this out.

"Well, baby. Do me a favor and keep me posted. I need to rest. Today has been a long day."

He agreed and we hung up. The door bell rang and startled me. I got up from the table and took a deep breath. I went to the door and paused before I opened it. *Do I really want to do this? I do still have love for him… maybe I should get his side of the story first,* I thought long and hard. The door bell rang again. I shook my thoughts, *No, you have to be strong, Kat. Think about how this man is holding your life up.* This was the only way I could move on. I opened the door and stepped aside so she could come in.

"Nice crib," she said as she inspected my place. She walked over to my dining room table, pulled out a chair, sat down, and crossed her well defined legs. "So, how can I help you, Tina?" she said in a business like tone.

I shut the door behind me and sat next to her at the table. I gave her a half smile. I never understood why she was the only one who called me Tina. No one did that, not even my mother. I studied her face. She wore no expression. She had a Chinese bob cut with honey brown highlights that complimented her skin. She had on a black cat suit adorned with rhinestones. She complimented it with a diamond cut choker and black stiletto rider boots.

"Did I interrupt you from anything? I mean, you seem a little over dressed," I said.

Fae blushed. "Well, let's just say I had to handle a little bit of business, and this was the proper attire for the festivities." She gave me a knowing look.

I was even more uncomfortable now. I could never understand how a beautiful girl such as herself could do what she did. Her demeanor really didn't fit her occupation. I decided to get straight to the point. I told her all about what Rashawn did to my sister and how I wanted him to disappear soon. She didn't say a word until I was finished. She went into her pocketbook and pulled out a blunt.

"Do you mind?" she asked.

I told her it was fine.

She sparked her blunt and went over to my couch. After a few pulls she said, "You know this won't be that easy… Mr. Gibbs is a very powerful man. We grew up together you know, so this is a little too close to home. Are you sure your sister is telling the truth?"

That question kind of caught me off guard. It had crossed my mind, but I knew she wouldn't lie on him like that. "Yeah, I know for a fact that it's true. She's laid up in the hospital having his baby as we speak!" I said. "And check this, he's with her… he doesn't know I know the truth. He thinks that I think the baby is Brock's." I laughed.

For some reason that didn't sit well with Fae, she choked off of her blunt. "What… who?" she said choking.

I repeated myself. "Kevin Brockman, you know… your foster brother who everyone thought was dead. Apparently he's not and Nalyse knew where he was. Matter of fact, he's supposed to be on his way up here as we speak."

Fae stood up and grabbed her phone out of her purse. She passed me the blunt and told me she would be right back. Before I could ask for an explanation she was out the door.

I sat there with my mouth open. *What just happened here?* I wondered. I shook my head and said, "Whatever."

I looked at the blunt. It was fat. I hadn't had any in a while so I decided to finish it off. Twenty minutes later I was laid out on the couch. I could barely open my eyes. My whole body felt like a ton of bricks as I tried to move. I heard Fae come back in the house. She took one look at me and laughed.

"I see you feeling real good, Tina. You looking awfully good too," she said.

I didn't notice that my robe was hanging open. I only had on a pair of pink bikini underwear underneath. I tried to cover up, but I couldn't move. She extended her hand and pulled me upright on the couch. I began to giggle.

"Thanks, was this weed laced?" I slurred.

She rolled her eyes. "What do you think?" she said.

I giggled again. "So are you going to kill that muva fucka, or am I gonna have to kill that nigga ma self?" I continued to slur. My speech was a mess. I couldn't control my words.

Fae smiled and patted my leg. She walked over to the bookshelf. I couldn't see what she was doing because my vision was blurred.

"Now about that… you know that's going to cost a few dollars right?" she asked.

"Money is not an issue. I have money saved up and my man has loot too," I told her.

She sat next to me. "I would normally charge about twenty thousand for man like Mr. Gibbs. I consider him to be my friend…my bestfriend."

She moved closer to me and put her hand on my thigh. She moved in even closer. I could feel her breath on my neck. I couldn't move. My body was numb.

"For you, I can do it for ten thousand; that is, if you let me play with your kitty kat. She moved her soft manicured hands and grasped my pouch.

Oh my God, what the hell is she doing? I thought. I got enough strength to move her hand. "I can't… I'll just pay the twenty thousand. I didn't know you were like that, Fae. I thought you messed with the Philly boy," I said. I was afraid of what was about to go down.

She smiled. "Baby, I ain't like that… I love me some dick, but I like kitty kat from time to time too. But if you ain't with it I understand, it's your choice."

She got up from my side and I was relieved. She stood there for a moment.

"You know what, Tina? We all have choices, and I don't think I want to take this job. Rashawn ain't never do shit to me. He's one of my best customers, so I think I am going to pass." She went to the table and collected her purse.

I was upset. *Why is she doing this? Is it because I won't give her any pussy?* I thought. I slid off the couch and on to my knees. I held the arm of the chair and pulled myself up.

"No… please… don't go… please wait," I begged.

She had made it halfway to the door. She turned around. I managed to stand up.

"Don't leave. I need you to do this for me. I'll pay and do anything. Just get rid of him," I begged.

She stared at me for a moment. "Anything?" she asked.

I opened my robe exposing my semi-nude body and let it fall to the floor. "Yes, anything," I replied.

Chapter 15
POISON

-Nalyse

"Ms. Nyse, sweetie, wake up," I heard a voice say.

I was already awake; I just couldn't open my eyes. I was in so much pain. It seemed like all through the night this white, fat ass nurse would come in pounding on my stomach. I cursed her ass out the last time she came in. I think that I hurt her little feelings, because she hadn't been in since. I felt heat run through my veins and then the pain subsided. Thank God for morphine. I opened my eyes and a pleasant face greeted me. She was a frail Hispanic lady. She looked as if she was in her mid-thirties.

"Hello. I need to press the air out of your abdomen."

She was so nice and gentle with me.

"Do you need anything?" she asked as she worked on my stomach.

"I'm starving," I admitted.

"I'll see what I can do to get you something to eat. Also, there is a gentleman in the waiting room waiting to see you. Do you feel like company?" she asked as she made her way to the door.

"Yes, that's fine." I was so excited. I knew it had to be Kevin.

I pulled the mirror out of my side drawer for a quick spruce up. My hair was a mess. I'd asked my mom to wrap it for me before I went into surgery. It just looked like a matted mess, swirled around my head. I combed it down and it looked like a big poof ball. I gave up. He would understand. I dabbed a little Vaseline on my lips. I heard the door opening so I threw everything in the drawer. I sat up in the bed and waited for my King.

If I could, I would have hauled ass. My face cringed in fear.

"Congratulations, mommy!" he said. He gave me a fake smile and planted a kiss on my lips. "Look at you, all grown up, looking all good and shit." Spinx squeezed my left tit and licked his lips. "Damn, baby, what you like… a double D now?"

He pulled a chair up and took my hand in his. I was dumbfounded. How in the hell did he know I was here? He sat there staring straight through me. He didn't say a word. He just kept smiling at me.

I broke the ice. "I had a little boy. He's in the NICU… he only weighed one pound and eleven ounces. He... he might not make it!" I began to cry.

The smile quickly faded from his face. He removed his hand and sat back in the chair. He was about to say something but, I cut him off.

"You know things have been real fucked up since you left… I was raped, my family turned against me… I had no choice, I…."

He jumped in. "Rape?" He laughed at me and waved his hand. "Nyse, cut the shit… you ain't get raped? Who… who raped you, Rashawn? I know you… remember that… I… know…you!" he reminded me.

He seemed to be a bit agitated. I realized I was going to have to switch shit up real quick. I had to think fast, because I knew he was going to make me pay for the shit I'd done. I had to make him feel sorry for me.

"No, Rashawn didn't rape me. He just took advantage of my situation. This is entirely your fault. The whole time you were busy playing house with Kita and Shay you left room for the enemy to sneak in." I had is attention now. "Remember Kevin? He's not dead. And guess what, he was setting you up the whole time. He used me. He acted like he really was into me only to get information about you. A few months after he disappeared he got in contact with me. He sent for me to come with him for a few days to get away. When I got there he treated me real nice. That is, until I started asking questions about you. I wanted him to tell me the truth if he set you up or not. He became enraged and started smacking me. He was callin' me names and said that I couldn't just leave well enough alone. Then… he raped me. He raped me because he was pissed that I still had love for you!"

Spinx got up from the chair and wrapped his arms around me. I felt wetness on my chest. I was grinning inside. His bitch ass was crying.

"I swear to God, I'm gonna kill that nigga!" he said.

I lifted his head off of me. "Baby, you can't do that. He's the father of my baby, not Rashawn. Rashawn is the only one who knows the truth, so please don't say anything to anyone, including my sister. I promise you when I get out of here I will help you bring both of them down. You just have to trust me… I love you, Spinx, baby."

I planted a hot passionate kiss on him and he melted in my hands. I couldn't believe he fell·for it. He promised me that he would hold off on doing anything to them. He gave me his new cell number and dropped me a few dollars. I promised that I would call him later. He asked if it was cool to go see the baby before he left. I told him he could and he was gone.

As soon as Spinx was out of sight, I called Kevin to see where he was at. He told me he was staying at the Embassy Suites and he would be here in about an hour. I told him about the visit I had with Spinx and how he threatened to kill me when I got out. He was heated. He told me he would have him handled ASAP. I told him to wait a minute because I knew a way we could kill two birds with one stone. He told me he loved me and he would see me soon, then we hung up. I shook my head in amazement and smiled.

I guess *Bell Biv DeVoe* had me in mind when they made that song "*Poison*." I knew I was wrong for the shit I was doing, but it was too late now. They deserved everything that was coming to them. Especially Rashawn, he had the nerve to be all hugged up with Kat while I was in pain having his damn baby. Every time I thought about it, it made me sick. His baby was fighting for his life, and he was probably somewhere having make-up sex with Kat. And I really couldn't wait to get a hold of that back stabbing ass Kee. She better cancel Christmas, 'cause that bitch wasn't making it.

I laughed to myself and said out loud, "Let the games begin!"

I buzzed the nurse to take me to see my son… Kevin Brockman Jr.

••••••••••••••••••••••••••••••••

I leaned over and kissed Little Kev's frail fingers. I hated leaving him here, but I had no choice, I was being discharged today. Big Kevin had been by my side since he'd come back. The little squabble he'd had with Rashawn a couple days ago still hadn't kept him away.

Speaking of Rashawn, I guess he was really pissed off at me. I asked the nurse if he had been back to visit the baby. She let me see sign-in sheet and the only names on it were both of our moms. I thought it was funny that just a week ago he was ecstatic about becoming a father, now he was no where to be found. *Oh well, he might as well not even start trying to be in the picture. It's not like he'll have much time to be in his life anyway,* I thought before handing her back the sign-in sheet.

I couldn't stand to see all those wires and machines hooked on my baby. I felt ill whenever I had to leave him. I think it was fear, I was afraid that it may be the last time I would see him. My tears started to fall. The nurse assured me that he was in good hands and he was a fighter. She told me to keep the bracelet on and I could come or call any time of day or night to check on him. She bent over and gave me a big hug, she was really nice. She gave Kevin a hug, too. I took one last look at Little Kev as Kevin wheeled me out of the room.

I cried the whole ride to my apartment. When we pulled up Kevin just sat there. I wiped my eyes.

"What's wrong, baby, why are you just sitting here?" I asked. I took the seatbelt off and sat up.

He just sat there with a blank look on his face for a minute. He finally turned to me and said, "Things are going to get better, you know that right?" Kevin had a sincere look of concern on his face.

"I know; I just can't wait until we are in Atlanta so we can start on our new life."

His facial expression changed to a smile. He walked me to the apartment door and waited for me to open it. I walked inside and he followed behind me. For some reason it just didn't feel the same. I thought I would be happy to be out of the hospital. A nagging feeling just kept taunting me.

Kevin brought my bags to my room and dropped them off. He gave me a quick kiss and said he had to go handle some business and he would call me when he was done. I forced a smile and gave him a hug. I went to the window and watched him drive off in his rental.

I took a deep breath and walked around the apartment. It didn't look like Rashawn had been here since I left. I went to the kitchen and picked up the phone to look at the caller ID. I didn't see anything unusual. I sat it back down and went to the bedroom. I checked the closets and drawers. All of his stuff was there still, untouched. *I bet that nigga is with my sister,* I thought. I stormed out the room and called Kat.

She answered on the first ring. "Hello." Her voice sounded real sketchy.

"That's real fucked up that you haven't been at the hospital to see your fuckin' nephew. He's in the N.I.C.U hooked to all these tubes and shit. But you don't care, because you're too busy having make-up sex with his fuckin' dad. How could you still fuck with him after he raped me? You know what? Fuck you… you selfish low life bitch!" I banged on her before she could even get a word in. I sat on the stool and waited for her to call back. To my surprise the phone never rang.

Chapter 16
MOMMY'S BABY DADDY'S MAYBE

-Fatal

I felt a tight squeeze around my waist, followed by soft wet kisses being placed on my neck. A mischievous smile spread across my face. I opened my eyes and scanned my bedroom. It was in total disarray. The sheets were now off the bed. My lamp was knocked over. The items on my bureau had found a new home all over the floor. I inched back and my ass was greeted by a massive weapon that was fully loaded and ready to let loose. Although I wanted him to unleash his power on me again; I decided against it. I pulled away and sat up in the bed. Rashawn had a confused look on his face.

I grabbed a sheet and wrapped it around my body, then walked over to my closet and pulled out my box of Philly's. I took a seat on my mahogany, leather Lay-Z-Boy recliner and opened the box to retrieve the bag of wet, my blade and a blunt. I needed my daily medicine so I could function throughout the day. I split the blunt open and dumped the tobacco out in the wastebasket. Out the corner of my eye I could see him rubbing on his meat. He was damn near drooling at the mouth, gazing at me. I shook my head in amazement. He was becoming a joke to me.

He had been staying here at my condo for the last two days. The first night I felt sorry for his ass. He'd called me crying and shit because he caught his new bitch lip locking with some other nigga after she'd just birthed his seed. And to make matters worse, she had the nerve to name the baby after dude. I asked him if he handled that and he told me that I just didn't understand. He gave me some lame excuse about how he could never hurt his son's mom and said there was more to it.

I warned him about little Ms. Nyse, just like I had warned my brother. Nyse was not to be trusted. She was young, spoiled and would do anything to get what she wanted. That was a dangerous combination; I should know. They should have known she was slimy. Shit, she fucked her sister's man, then had the audacity to get pregnant and play house with the nigga. Then there's the shit she did to Spinx, she fucked him royally. The crazy thing is Spinx still didn't know she was the one who snitched on him. If he did I know he would have had me handle her ass a long time ago.

I chuckled to myself. I had to admit she was bad little bitch. With the right guidance, that bitch could be deadly. She was a far cry from her bitch ass sister. I couldn't stand that bitch, and if it wasn't for Rashawn I would have merked her back in the eighth grade!

Now back to Ra-Ra. I knew he was hurt, and I couldn't just leave him out there like that. He had been my friend since the second grade. He was my first love, and we had been fucking off and on since I was like twelve. He loved fucking me because he could let all of his frustrations out. That's the way I loved it, rough and violent. That's the only way I could get my rocks off with a man. I had feelings for him that no one could understand, but I hated him at the same time for choosing her over me.

I was there before the infamous Kat came on the scene. She was a trip, too. I remember when her ass was "Dusty Tina" from Bennett Street. Ra-Ra was the best thing that could have happened to her whole family. He's the reason why her mom was able to buy that house in Serenity Hills. Now all of a sudden she thinks she's hot shit and unattainable. I had to laugh at that one.

The look on her face when I told her she had to give me some head was priceless. Tears dropped from her eyes right before she got lost in my chasm. I had to admit, she was pretty good for a beginner. When I pulled out "Rick the Dick" I thought the bitch was going to faint. I bent that bitch over the couch and went to work on her. For a minute there I thought she liked the shit. She was deeply moaning and clawing at the furniture. That just pissed me off more. I wasn't trying to please her. I wanted her to feel the pain. She's the reason why Ra and I weren't together today. He was my first and he left me for that bitch.

He always said he looked at me like one of his boys. I guess I couldn't blame him for thinking that way. I was cute, but I was a late bloomer. I was rough and ran with some of the hardest niggas out there. I was running up in cribs and some more shit. Then the ultimate happened, I hated thinking about it. That's the night FATAL was birthed.

I had to shake it off. I was beginning to get in my feelings. I passed the blunt to Ra, who was now getting dressed. He waved off my offering. This didn't do anything but piss me off. I rolled my eyes in disgust.

"Where you about to go?" I said dryly.

He didn't say anything, just kept getting dressed with this sour look on his face.

"Oh, what… you mad now because I ain't feel like giving your punk ass no pussy? Is that it?" I rose to my feet and stood in his way. I took a pull off my blunt and with the other hand I poked him in his forehead. "What, are you deaf now mutha fucka? I asked your bitch ass a question… I expect a fuckin' answer. Are you mad 'cause I ain't give you none of my pussy?"

His nostrils began to flare. I was getting to his ass. He tried to go around me, but I wouldn't let him pass. The muscles in his arms began to tighten, but I wasn't worried. I knew his ass wasn't crazy. I laughed wickedly and flicked my ashes on his chest. He bit his lip while balling up his fist. I felt my pussy getting wet. I hauled off and punched him in his face. When I did that my sheet fell, exposing my naked body.

"What, nigga? You gonna hit me now?" I tagged him again.

He backed up away from me.

"What, you want some pussy… huh, nigga?" I pushed him on the bed.

He lay back as I climbed on top of his face and spread eagle. He gripped my thighs and pulled me down over his mouth. Within seconds my body began to quiver. He really knew how to put it on me. He was using his tongue between my ass and pussy, making me cum repeatedly. When he was finished he had my thick white juices all around his mouth. He smiled proudly when he noticed how weak I was. I could barely crawl off of him. Being the bitch I am, I couldn't let him think he got the best of me.

I slyly said, "It was all right, but you need to get some lessons from your bitch Kat, her head game is on point. Matter of fact, this may help."

I slid to the side of my bed and opened the drawer to my nightstand. I pulled out a video tape and threw it on his lap. He sat there looking stupid. I sighed and took the tape and popped it in my VCR. When the TV came on his mouth dropped open when he saw his precious Kat plotting his murder, then fucking me in his house. I had her ass so high that night she didn't even notice me setting the camera up on her bookshelf. I felt bad when I saw that nigga cry, but I had to let him know what was going down.

I told him everything about Nyse telling her sister he raped her and how Kat was the one who hired niggas to kill him at the graduation. I even threw some other shit in there to piss him off. I lied and said Nyse was fucking my brother the whole time and Brock really was the father. I wanted those bitches gone. That was the only way he would agree with it.

-Kat

I stood there looking at the phone. I couldn't believe her. I couldn't even fathom why she would think I would mess with him after what he did to her. I sat up in bed and hung up the phone. I felt a headache coming on. I grabbed the bottle of Jack off my nightstand and gulped it down. I ran my hands through my hair and lay back.

These last few days had been the worst I'd ever experienced in my life. I hadn't talked to Allen in days. I was supposed to go away with him next week to his parent's house to celebrate Easter. He called and even stopped by, but I just ignored him. After the fifth day he finally gave up. Then there was Fae. That Bitch had been coming over on a regular basis ever since the night she forced herself on me. I felt like a whore every time she touched me. I would force myself to throw-up after every encounter.

This shit had to stop. I just wanted her to hurry up and handle Rashawn so she could leave me the hell alone. The sooner he was gone, the sooner I would be able to have my life back. A sudden sentiment of guilt came over me. I thought about my nephew and how he was fighting for his life. I was so wrapped up in my own shit that I hadn't thought about him.

I immediately got up to shower. I was going to meet my nephew, because if something happened I would never be able to forgive myself. After I was dressed, I decided to call Nalyse. The phone rang for a while, and the answer machine picked up. I left her a message apologizing for not being there. I assured her that I would be a better aunt and I was on my way to see my nephew now. After I hung up, I grabbed my coat and opened the door. I ran smack into Rashawn's chest.

"Where are you in a rush to?" he asked. Rashawn stood in front of me with his hands in his Girbaud jeans, staring me down.

All types of different emotions ran through me at the sight of him. I wanted to grab something and bust his head open, then I wanted to run into his arms and let him hold me like he used to. I didn't want to tell him shit. But I still had to play nice. His day was coming soon anyway.

"I'm going to the hospital; you want to come with me? He's your nephew, too."

He looked at me funny and said, "Naw, that's cool, but make sure you come straight back because we need to talk." He walked past me into my house.

I was baffled. This nigga never came to my house and now he was freely walking in it. "Baby, what are you doing?" I asked. I followed behind him inside.

He made himself at home. He was making his way up the steps.

"Rashawn, where are you going?" I demanded.

He stopped in his tracks and turned back towards me. "What the fuck you mean what am I doing? Is there some reason why I can't be in the fucking house that I pay for?" he snapped.

He was coming towards me at a fast pace with a very unpleasant look on his face. I didn't know what to expect. I knew damn well he wasn't gonna hit me, at least I hoped he wasn't. We were now standing toe to toe. His eyes were filled with anguish. I couldn't look at him. I directed my attention to the cream carpet. His tone changed and he became very sweet all of a sudden.

"Kat, baby, why you acting like that… you don't want me here… I thought you were my Queen. Don't you remember, Together Forever?" He massaged the back of my neck and pulled me into his chest.

Together forever? That phrase alone brought back memories that I'd tried to hide deep within. That was our song, the song that played the night he proposed to me at my senior prom. Those where the words that we spoke to each right before we said, I love you. I wanted to break away and tell him what I knew, how I hated him and how I wish he would disappear forever. Something inside me wouldn't let me break away. I actually felt safe in his arms, despite all that he had done. A tingling sensation went down my spine as he whispered sweet nothings in my ear. I was getting lost in my emotions.

"Are you still my Queen?" he asked me again.

I wished I could have had an outer body experience so I could have kicked my damn self in the mouth for what was about to fly out of it. "Yes, I am... and you're my King," whimpered.

"Together Forever, Katty?"

My tears dropped on his chest. I loved this man, and no matter how much I tried to fight it, I needed him in a malignant way. There was no way I could let Fae carry out her plan. I finally came to the realization that if he died, a huge part of me would die, too. He was my lifeline, my soul mate. "Yes, Together forever," I replied.

That's all it took. Before I knew it, I was on my back with my legs up. I guess you can't help who you love. Needless to say, I never made it to go see my nephew.

••••••••••••••••••••••••••••••••••

Rashawn had moved in and things were getting back to how they used to be. Well, sort of. He would still disappear some nights and come home bright and early in the morning. What really amazed me was Fae. It seemed like as soon as Rashawn came back home she hadn't tried to make any contact with me. I wasn't complaining, but I needed to talk to her because I wanted her to drop her plans against Rashawn. The more time we spent together, the more suspicion I had about my sister's story. Something just wasn't right.

One afternoon my mother came over to the house. She looked really upset. We sat down and talked for a while and that's when I found out that Mrs. Gibbs was visiting the baby. My mother said she went to visit Little Kevin and they wouldn't let her in. She asked the nurse why not; she went every day after work and never had an issue before. The nurse said they were performing a test on the baby and no one could go back there at that time. She told her that she could wait in the waiting room until they were finished, so she decided to do just that.

She said about twenty minutes later Rashawn and his mother came out with the doctor. At this point she was really confused. She went to ask why they were allowed back there and they were no relation to the baby, but by time she got to them Rashawn and his mother were walking away. She was going to stop them, but something told her not to. She asked the doctor if everything was ok. Since he knew her, he told her they had just finished taking a DNA test and for her not to worry. He went on to say that there were no needles used they just needed to swab his cheek.

She told me she tried to call Nalyse and ask her what was going on, but she cursed her out and hung up. I didn't know what to say. I hated the way things always fell on me. What was I supposed to say… that he raped her daughter? Then she would hate me and try to have him arrested or something. I closed my eyes and took a deep breath.

"Mom, I don't know how to say this, but Lil' Kevin is actually Rashawn's son."

She burst out into tears.

"Mom, don't cry. It was a misunderstanding. I umm, I cheated on Rashawn, and he found out. As a matter fact, he actually caught me in the act, I just didn't know it. It seems that him and Nalyse met up and went for a couple of drinks and one thing led to another." I didn't expect what was coming next. She hauled off and slapped me dead in my face.

"How could you do that to him? After all he's done for us, you go and sleep with someone behind his back? I can't blame him for his mistake, but I tell you what… I know that conniving ass sister of yours knew what she was doing! I can't believe this! What type of children do I have that you're so unappreciative?" She grabbed her purse and stormed out.

I sat there dumfounded. That's when I decided it was time for me to find out his side of the story. I just needed to get the courage to come clean on my end.

Chapter 17
SETTING THINGS IN ORDER

-Nalyse

Things were not going the way I planned. Two weeks had passed since I saw Rashawn. He came in the day after I was discharged talking stupid. I was sitting in the living room on the phone playing nice with Caree. I was trying to get information on Kee's whereabouts. She said she heard she was going down south somewhere, but hadn't heard exactly where. It was cool, because I was gonna find that bitch and make her pay.

Caree gave me the latest gossip on what was going on in the Hills. Of course Spinx's surprise return was the hot topic out there. I couldn't get the entire scoop because this nigga was staring me all in the mouth, so I told her I would call her back. He sat on the love seat in front of me with a smug look on his face.

"Oh, so now you finally decide to show up. Why haven't you been to see your son?" I snapped. I really didn't give two shits if he saw him or not. I was just playing the part.

He just kept giving me this look, like he was disgusted or

something.

"What, nigga, Kat got your fuckin' tongue? I asked you a question," I snapped.

I didn't even see it coming. I found myself on the floor with his thick ass hands around my throat. I thought my damn heart was in my throat. I gasp and wiggled trying to get from under him.

"I could kill your little ass right now, and I bet no one would miss you! I know what you told Kat. I raped you? Bitch, I ain't need to rape you. You threw me the pussy and then sold her out. What do you think she's gonna do when she finds out you been snitchin' on her the whole time? Do you know how much shit you done started?" he growled, banging my head on the floor. "Do you?" He let go of my throat and stood up.

I began coughing uncontrollably and gagging. Tears welded up in my eyes. I wished I had something to hit that nigga with, because I would have fucked him up. I sat up, trying to catch my breath. He paced back and forth.

"I'm only gonna ask you this once… is that my fucking baby? Please don't lie, because I'm gonna get a test anyway. And if it turns up that it ain't mine, I am gonna kill you myself. I can't believe that I allowed you to do this to me, to leave the only person I ever loved. I never loved you… you do know that right? You were just her replacement. I mean, if I couldn't have her anymore why not have the next best thing, the sister. You know we're back together right? Your little lie backfired. She fuckin' hates you. She never wants to see you again, so stop calling and harassing her! She wants nothing to do with you! You're dead to her!"

Every word he spat stung like venom. I was so mad. *How could she have told him? She promised me she wouldn't say anything,* I thought. I couldn't blame her for being mad at me, but hate, come on, I was her only sister. This shit just wasn't worth it. Rashawn sat on the couch next to me. He pulled me by my hair until I was off the floor. I cried in pain.

"What the fuck are you crying for? You did this shit to yourself. Now this is how shit is gonna work. You are going to get the DNA test. If that baby is mine, his name is getting changed and you're signing custody over to me and my mother. There is no way I'm going to let a heartless bitch like you raise my seed. You understand that? You will never, ever, see my son again. So you can pack up your bags and go live with that faggot ass nigga Kev. Y'all deserve each other." He stood up and walked towards the door. "Oh, by the way, I heard you had set up shop behind my back out in the Hills, I want my fucking cut. You got thirty days. If you ain't got it, I suggest you get missing, ASAP. I'll give you a head start before I come looking," he spat. He slammed the door as he left out.

I ran to the door and locked the bolt on it. I went to the bathroom and examined myself. Bruises in the replica of his fingers were appearing on my neck. I picked up the comb and ran it through my hair, clumps of it fell out. I screamed and threw a jar of Liv into the mirror, cracking it. *What happened? Where did I go wrong?* I thought. This was supposed to go smoothly but it was dwindling downhill rapidly. I looked at myself in the mirror. My reflection was out of wack because of the crack. That's how I felt. There was a crack somewhere in my life. I just needed to figure out how to piece it back together.

That's how it went down between us. Now two weeks later I was sitting here alone in this apartment trying to figure what I need to do to fix this. I told Kevin what Rashawn did, but he didn't give me the response I'd wanted. He was real calm and cool about it, talking some mess about he will handle it, but now was just not the time. *Now is just not the time?* I thought. *What fucking time is better than now?*

Rashawn damn near knew everything that was going on. He just didn't know what part Kevin played in it. I was getting to the point to where I didn't know either. I'd barely saw him since I'd been home. He kept telling me that he was trying to make sure things were going to go smoothly for us, but I wasn't trying to hear that shit. I did what I should have done in the first place, called the one person I knew would handle my problem.

Spinx had stopped by a few times a week, making sure I had cash and something to eat. Of course he wanted something in return. I couldn't give him any ass yet, but I had other ways of pleasing him. He wanted to go kill Rashawn when I told I him what he did to me. I wanted him to do it, too. But I knew there was something huge I would be missing out on if I reacted too quickly.

Rashawn thought he had a huge shipment coming in next week. Something was coming but it wasn't what he thought. He was supposed to finally meet his connect face to face, because this deal was just too big to handle through UPS. He had been preparing for this shipment for some time, and I knew he was damn near using every penny he had for this supply.

Rashawn didn't know I knew about it. He tried to do it on the side. The funny thing is, I knew every move he made with the connect, because his connect was Kevin. I couldn't wait to see his face when he found out. At first I didn't really want to see his demise, but after he turned my sister against me and put his hands on me; I wanted to see that rotten bastard take his last breath.

I was peeking out the window when I noticed the mailman pulling off. I decided to go check the mail. I was waiting for

Lil' Kevin's insurance papers to come. It was starting to get hot outside. I opened my box and the first thing that caught my eye was a letter from Kee. *No that bitch didn't write me*, I thought. I looked at the address and it was marked Raleigh, North Carolina. I opened it up and began to read it.

She was kicking some shit about how she changed her life and that she accepted God. I had to laugh. *I know this bitch is tripping now... God, come on,* I thought. She didn't have a religious bone in her body. I read on, shaking my head in disbelief. She was inviting me to come and stay with her and her cousin. She was crazy, I would be down there, but it damn sure wouldn't be to stay and play church with her ass. I was coming to wreak havoc, so she better be prayed up.

When I walked in my house I heard the phone ringing. I ran to it and Spinx was on the line. "Hey, baby," I said seductively.

We chit chatted for a while and he asked if we could spend time together this weekend at the mote. I thought about it for a minute. It had been a while since I had some and I wasn't bleeding anymore. So I told him it was a date.

-*Kat*

"I really enjoyed our evening out," I whispered in Rashawn's ear.

We were cuddled up on the rug in front of the fireplace. Of course it wasn't lit because we would have burned the hell up. It was the middle of spring, and we had just returned from an evening of dancing and dining at Zanzibar Blue in Philly. Afterwards, we came back here and he commenced to giving me the best sex I'd ever had. I was in heaven. I lay in his arms staring at his dreamy eyes. I loved this man, I really did. My mother was right; he had been there for not only me, but my entire family. I owed him the truth.

I closed my eyes and whispered, "Would you ever do anything to hurt me?"

He kissed me on the forehead. "You're my every thing and you know that. I would never do anything to harm you, the question is would you do anything to harm me?" he asked gently.

I propped my head up on my arm and ran my hand down his bare chest. I lay there thinking, *did he just ask me what I think he did*? He sat up and pulled me close to him. I was afraid to answer the question, but I knew I had no choice. I looked up at him directly in his soft brown eyes. "I can't lie to you baby, lately… due to certain circumstances… I wished you were out of my life. I even thought about ways to be free from you," I confessed.

He had a confused look on his face. "What circumstances? What are you talking about, Kat?"

"There's something I need to ask you, and I need the truth. Did you rape Nalyse, and are you Little Kevin's dad?"

Rashawn took a deep breath and placed his hands behind his head. "First of all, I would never do anything to hurt anyone in your family… rape… you and I both know I don't need to rape anyone. Now, did I have sex with Nalyse; I made a mistake and had sex with her. It happened the night of her graduation. She came to thank me for the truck. She told me that you were sleeping with a guy named Allen from your school and that he was living here in my house. Of course I was upset. She played on my emotions and one thing led to another, and we were in the bed. After that night she thought it was going to be a regular thing, but I told her I wasn't interested. She started threatening me, saying she was going to tell you that we were fucking if I didn't keep her tightened up or break her off from time to time. I would have been told you, but I saw you with that nigga at the movies. You looked like you was in love, so I just let you do your thing. Next thing I know she comes running to me saying she's pregnant. So, I put her in an apartment and made sure she was taken care of. But is the baby mine? I'm not even sure. I took a DNA test since that nigga Kevin came back in the picture," he said.

I couldn't believe what I was hearing. That was nowhere close to what she had told me. I felt so ashamed for my actions in the past year. I wished I could have taken it all back, but it was too late.

I snuggled on his chest and apologized, "I am so sorry about Allen… I was so lonely, you were always gone and I was so unhappy. I knew you were hustling to take care of us, but I needed more, I needed you. Lyse, I can't believe she lied to me. She told me you raped her. I love you so much, but why couldn't you just have come to me? We could have worked through this." I cried.

Rashawn rubbed my back. "It's going to be ok. I know that you're sorry. Everything is going to be fine, sooner than you think."

-Fatal

This nigga was always late. I looked at my Rolex, and the time read 10:20 pm. This nigga was supposed to be here damn near an hour ago. I sipped on my Merlot and enjoyed the scenery.

This sexy, fine ass Spanish dude kept giving me the eye. He looked caked up, too. He had on a charcoal colored Armani suit with some Gators to match. I gave him a little smile and he winked. We had been playing this game for the last twenty minutes. He was at a table with a few other gentlemen who also wore expensive gear. To the regular crowd they would have looked like business men, but I knew the deal. Those niggas were most definitely making underground power moves.

The waiter asked me if I needed anything else. I told him I was fine, and he slipped me a folded up piece of paper. I opened it up, and it was from Mr. Armani. His name was Miguel Diaz, he dropped me his digits. I looked in his direction and gave him a nod of approval. He gave me a big grin, and that's when I noticed his deep dimples.

Damn, he's fine, I thought. I looked him over. From the looks of it, he looked like he could do a little damage in the bedroom. Those Spanish niggas were crazy, too, just how I like them, a little deranged. Just when I was about to get deep into my little day dream I was interrupted by this ignorant ass nigga.

"What's up, baby. I see you over there checking out Chico and shit," he joked.

Spinx black ass came strolling in damn near an hour late wearing this loud turquoise, leather Avirex Jacket; a pair of Fendi shades; and a black Gap sweat suit. He was the only person I knew who could pull some shit off like that and still think he looked good.

"Nigga, you know you wrong for coming here all late. I was getting ready to leave this bitch. You are paying for my fucking drinks, too." I added. I tried to act like I was pissed. But I couldn't hold it in any longer, I had to laugh. I couldn't get pass that bright ass jacket on his fool ass.

"What, what's so fucking funny, Fae?" he said while cheesing. He knew damn well what I was laughing at.

"Nigga, you, you and that Gymboree looking jacket, nigga. That shit looks ridiculous and you know it."

He started laughing. "Fuck you, Fae, with your stankin' ass… look, everything is set up for this weekend. I just need you to show up and scare the shit out of her ass. I want her to know I ain't playing with her ass. I mean, I got mad love for her, but she play to damn much. I feel like Samson found my weak point and sent the enemy in to devour me. But I can't lie, I love that little bitch. She's devious as a mother fucka, but I love me some Nyse! I just need to get her ass in check, even if I have to make her stare death in the face to get her ass right," he said, taking my glass of merlot to the head.

I shook my head in amazement. This chick had all three of those niggas going bananas. I didn't know what type of voodoo she had going on, but they were lost under her spell. I thought Rashawn had put her in her place, but a few days afterwards he was feeling some type of way. She wasn't my concern any way; I had other plans for her.

I had to make him come to his senses. I couldn't believe when he told me he was going to let Kat get away with trying to kill him. I told him he had to be fucking nuts. She needed to be an example; no one would respect him if it got out that he let that shit go. How much more was he gonna let her get away with? If I had my way, which I eventually would, that bitch would be history by the end of the week.

Spinx and I sat around talking shit until we were both pissy drunk. We both staggered out of the restaurant holding on to one another. I could barely stand up.

"Yo, Fae, you all right?" he slurred. I noticed his truck was parked closer to the entrance than mine. I guess his punk ass didn't want to walk me to my ride.

"Yeah, nigga, I'm cool. I'm just a few rows away." We gave each other a pound and went our separate ways. Not even a minute later I heard him peel off. *Damn, he didn't even wait to see if I made it safely,* I thought. *But who the fuck in their right mind would fuck with me? I'm Fatal!*

I took my heels off so I could have better balance. Halfway to my car I felt something all too familiar poking me in my side. *Wow, I know this shit is not happening to me now.* I thought. The only thing I could do was laugh. I'd got caught slipping. I tried to turn around to see who finally caught up with me, but they pressed the barrel deeper in my side.

"I don't want to hurt you. I just want to talk business."

That voice was familiar. They removed the gun from my side. I laughed as I turned around to greet this brave soul. I couldn't believe that standing in front of me toting a nickel plated .357 magnum was the infamous Nyse. She stood there staring me straight in the eyes, studying my every move. She had the gun in her right hand, pressed against her thigh. *Hmm. Let me see how much heart she really got*, I thought. I lounged towards her. She swiftly had the gun aimed towards my skull. She even had the nerve to cock it back.

"I told you, Fae, I want to do business. I'm not trying to hurt you. Let's take a walk to your car so we can talk," she said, still aiming the gun at my head.

I couldn't believe this shit. I couldn't stop smiling. This bitch was really bout it. I turned around and walked to my car. She followed behind me. When we reached my car, I got in. I unlocked the passenger side door to let her in. She went around to the back door and sat behind me. *Good girl,* I thought. I just wondered where she learned all this shit from.

"So, what's up, Ms. Nyse, what can I do for you?"

"I know your brother has his plans for Rashawn, but he's taking too long. He needs to be dealt with ASAP. He knows that I've been stealing from him, and he threatened to kill me. It won't be long before he finds out about the connect being fake. He's on some other shit now, and he threatened to take my son."

I sat and listened to her whole little plan. I had to admit, it was well thought out. Of course the money that she gave to me upfront was lovely.

"There's more where that came from. I know that Rashawn has more at my sister's, and she has a secret safe in her walls. If you do this for me in a timely manner you can have everything that's in there," she said.

It sounded good, but something was just not quite piecing together. "So, what's in it for you? I know you want more than just this nigga in the dirt. You don't want no loot?"

She smiled at me in a weird freaked out sort of way.

"No, I don't want any money him, six feet under is enough." She opened the car door and slid out. Before she walked away she turned to me. "Oh, Fae, just to let you know, Rashawn has $250,000 bounty on Kevin's head. Not to be in your business, but whatever is up between you and Spinx, you need to cut it off. He's the nigga that plans to put the bullets in Kev's head. Within seconds she had disappeared back into the night.

Chapter 18
LOST ONES

-Nalyse

I was so excited. Little Kevin had gotten up to three pounds and eleven ounces and he was now off of the ventilator. I bawled my eyes out as I held my baby in my hands for the first time. I rubbed his little peanut head and fed him his formula through the syringe. My baby was strong, just like his mother.

I played with his tiny feet and hands and rocked in the chair. I told him how things were going to be so good for us and how we were gonna go far away from everybody. No one was ever gonna take him away from me. I wouldn't allow it. I held him as close to me as I possibly could. I was so caught up into my mommy mode that I didn't realize my mom had walked in.

"Oh my God! They let you hold him!" she exclaimed. She had her hands over her mouth, and tears appeared in her eyes.

I smiled happily. "Yeah, he's three pounds and eleven ounces; they said he's breathing on his own now. He just needs a little oxygen… you want to hold him?"

She nodded eagerly. I carefully passed him to her. She had to fight back her tears of joy. She kissed on him and sang little silly songs. It was nice watching her bound with him. I couldn't help but notice she never gave me any eye contact when she talked to me. I guess she was still pissed at me for cursing her out. I hadn't meant to, but she called at the wrong time. Too much shit was going on, and she called questioning me about some damn paternity test.

With her eyes glued on Lil' Kevin she said, "Did you get the test results back?"

I knew it was too good to be true. I sat back in the chair and exhaled. "Mom, look, I know I should have just told you the truth, but I didn't know what to say. If you want to know if Rashawn is his father, the answer is yes. He is biologically Little Kevin's dad, but he will not be raising him. Kevin and I will; that's why I opted to name him after Kevin. I could see the fire in her eyes. I knew she wanted to go off, but wasn't in the right place for it.

She started on me anyway. "Lyse, I don't know what to say about you. God knows you need to get yourself together. Do you think before you do these things? Seriously, what goes through that mind of yours? What happened to you? Where did I go wrong as a mother? I pray everyday and ask God why? Why did I get stuck with these heathen children? I… I… just don't know." She sniffled and handed me Lil' Kevin. "I just hope that you get yourself together before this child comes home. He needs special care, Lyse, he's fragile. Promise me you'll take care of him, and if you can't do it, give him to someone who can provide the love and care he needs." She gave him a kiss and told him she loved him and left.

I felt a huge lump in my throat. I loved my mother, I really did. I just didn't think she loved me. Or was it that she didn't love the person I had become? I looked at the clock and it was 3 pm. I had been here since this morning. I had to get ready to go. Spinx was picking me up at 9 pm to stay with him for the weekend. I gave my baby a kiss and hurried out.

I called Kevin on the way to my car to tell him the good news. He was happy to hear it. He apologized for not coming to the hospital with me, but he had to tie up a few loose ends before the shipment. He asked what I was doing later, and I told him I was hanging out with Caree for the weekend. He told me to have fun and stay out of trouble. We said I love you and hung up.

-Kat

I finally got a chance to speak with Fae. I was furious. I told her I had been trying to get in touch with her for weeks. She told me she had been busy putting in work. I knew what that meant, so I didn't ask any questions. I told her we needed to talk because I didn't want her to follow through with our plans. She gave me a bunch of lip, talking about she already spent the money and all this other mess. I told her I wasn't worried about that. She wanted to know why. I told her we were back together and we were getting married in June. She fell silent for a moment. She told me to meet her at the Ramada Inn tonight at 9:30 pm. She said she would call me later with the room number. I had a feeling I wasn't going to like what she had in store, but I guess the same way I got into this mess would be the same way I got out.

-Fatal

"Fae you are one hot deadly bitch!" I said out loud.

I was admiring myself in the mirror. I'd just stepped out of the shower to get ready for this evening's festivities. I decided on wearing my black, lace thong and bra set. It was sexy and the right color for tonight's theme. There was definitely going to be some mourning going on. I sparked up my herbal medication and popped a Zanny. I chased it with a shot of Henny.

I wore my Dior halter cat suit with a pair of black Dior fuck me pumps. I gave Rashawn a quick call to remind him about our date tonight. I talked to my little brother to let him know everything was going down tonight, and I needed him to meet me in the parking garage. I made sure my baby "Nina" was safely tucked in my oversized Dior bag with a few other goodies. Thanks to Nyce, I was gonna have a nice fat stash. I didn't know how she was gonna feel about me after I was done with Kat. I figured she shouldn't be too mad, it's not like she really cared about her anyway. I'd just make it look like it was all Spinx's doing, just so she didn't trip. But if she did, I would take care of her, too. I applied some lip gloss and mascara before I flat ironed my hair. I took another shot of Henny for the road and left. I was getting hungry, and my appetite was for destruction.

••••••••••••••••••••••••••••••••

-Nalyse

I brushed my hair back in a sleek ponytail. I tried to wrap it, but the bald spot Rashawn made was showing. Just the thought of him made me want to cut his fuckin' throat. I shook it off. "Nyse, you are going to enjoy yourself this weekend. No worries," I kept telling myself.

I looked myself over and noticed that I had gained a hell of a lot of weight. My hips had spread and my tits were spilling over my bra. I had to be about a triple D. Just to think, bitches paid to get tits like this. It was awkward looking; they could have them. My stomach was going down nicely. If only I could get the hips, tits, and thighs tight I would be good again.

I grabbed my overnight bag from the bed and went into the kitchen. I poured myself a glass of lemonade and sorted through my mail. There were two letters that caught my interest. One was from the Division of Social Services, and the other was from Kee. I opened up the Social Services letter first. It was the DNA results. 99.98%. I smiled. *To bad he won't be around to see this,* I thought, as I placed it in my purse.

I opened Kee's letter. I read half of it and threw it in my bag. She was on her Jesus saves kick again. I would save that for when I needed to be entertained. I heard the horn blow outside. I looked out the window and saw it was Spinx. I gathered my things and ran to his truck.

I hopped in and gave him a kiss. "Where are we going?" I asked while I fastened my seat belt.

"The Ramada Inn," he replied.

I smiled, I was happy that she'd stuck with the plan.

•••••••••••••••••••••••••••••••••

Isn't this ironic, I thought as I looked out the window. Our room overlooked the cemetery. "This is cute, a graveyard, wow, how fuckin' romantic," I complained.

He ignored me and turned the TV on. "What you want to

eat?" he asked.

"I don't care. I'm not hungry," I said as I lay across the bed.

He playfully smacked my ass. "You got donkey booty now. That shit's shaking like jelly."

I didn't know if I should take that as a compliment or not. He started tugging at my jeans until he got them down. I turned over on my back and he pulled them off. He took his shirt and pants off and pulled my T-shirt off. His eyes nearly popped out of his head when he saw my breast. He began to feast on them immediately. I thought I was going to die from the pain, because my tits were still tender and swollen. He was sucking so hard that the milk began to flow out. He removed my panties and was about to go to work.

I stopped him dead in his tracks. "No, nigga, you will not be going up in me raw," I said.

He looked at me like I was crazy.

"Boy, I'm serious. If you ain't got a rubber this shit ain't happening."

He sat up on the side of the bed and was about to get something out of his pocket, until his cell phone rang. He looked at the number and went into the bathroom. I had to laugh. *It never fails,* I thought. I pulled my panties up and put my jeans on.

"What are you doing?" he asked when he came back out.

"I want to leave, I want to go back home," I replied.

He sucked his teeth. "It's not what you think. I have to make a run, I'll be right back."

I continued to protest, but he wasn't hearing it. He got dressed and told me he would be back in a half. He left me just like that, I couldn't believe it. I went to the bathroom to pee. While I was in there I heard the door open. I thought it was Spinx coming back. I was about to flush the toilet when

I heard a female's voice. I cracked the door open and that's when I found out the voice belonged to my sister.

What is she doing here? I thought. I was about to go and say something until I heard another female. I could hear her voice, but I couldn't see her. I shut the door back and looked around for a vent or something. There was a small walk in closet inside the bathroom. I opened the door and noticed a nice size vent on the floor. I lay down on the floor, cramming myself inside. I could see the bed clearly.

I heard Kat say, "If we do this you have to promise me this will be the last time and you'll call the hit off."

I saw another set of female legs directly in front of the vent blocking my view. I heard the female say, "I promise; this will be the *last* time."

I didn't like the way she said that. She stressed the word "last" too much for me. The legs moved out of my way and she made her way towards the bed. Kat began to undress while she watched. I couldn't believe what was going on. Was my sister ready to fuck this chick and for what? The female still had her back towards me as she stripped down to nothing.

The female then lay on the bed while Kat climbed on top of her and spread her legs open. I couldn't watch what happened next. I heard a bunch of slurping and moaning. I thought I was going to be sick. I tried to figure out what the hell was going on and why they were in my hotel room. I began to panic. *What the fuck is going on. Fae will be here any minute with Rashawn and where is Spinx. He should have been back by now,* I thought. My mind was going every which way. I tried to focus on what my sister was doing. She had to get the fuck out of there. Some serious shit was about to go down, and she was about to fuck it all up.

I heard the door open again, and I heard Rashawn's voice.

"What the fuck is this shit!" he yelled.

Kat jumped from between the girl's thighs. Her mouth had sticky shit all around it. She looked at the female on the bed and became hysterical. "You set me up! I'll kill you… you fuckin' dyke bitch."

The mystery female sat up in the bed packing a .9 millimeter in her hand. My mouth dropped when I noticed that it was Fatal. I had sick feeling come over me. This was not gonna end pretty. This bitch had thrown some salt in the game. This was not the plan. I had no idea she was fucking with Kat. I had to do something; that was my sister out there and he was definitely going to kill her after witnessing this shit. I tried to think fast, but nothing was coming to me quick enough.

Rashawn grabbed Kat and told her to get her clothes on then turned his attention to Fatal. "Fae, what are you doing? I told you to leave her the fuck alone. What the fuck is wrong with you?" He was infuriated.

Fae still had the gun aimed at Kat. *What the fuck is she doing? That shit is supposed to be on Rashawn*, I thought. I could have sworn that bitch started to twitch. She had her eyes on Kat, but her attention was on Rashawn.

"You still taking up for this bitch after all she did? She tried to kill you, not once but twice. She was fucking another nigga and me, she's rotten. You parade this bitch around calling her a fucking Queen. Got mother fuckers in the streets bowing down to this bitch, breaking their neck to meet her every need. She ain't shit! All she has ever done was take, take and take some more from you! Then her little clone comes into your life and plays the hell out of you. Did you know she's been setting you up? No… you didn't. You're so fucked up over Queen Kat that you didn't even notice Nyse basically snatched your business right from under your nose," she taunted.

I sat there rocking back and forth, anxious. I was trying to figure out what to do next. *This bitch is crazy. What the fuck is wrong with her?* I thought. I listened to Fae's every word. I couldn't believe it. This bitch was jealous of Kat, and she had a thing for Rashawn. *Ain't that a bitch, she used me,* I thought. Rashawn and Fae began to argue back and forth. I slowly inched out of the closet. As soon as I opened the bathroom door I heard a ping type noise from the silencer.

I watched in horror as Kat slowly dropped to the floor. I tried to scream, but nothing would come out. Thick, dark red blood leaked out of the small hole that penetrated Kat's forehead. Rashawn rushed Fae and knocked the gun from her hand. I grabbed my chest in anguish at the site of my lifeless sister. I dropped to the floor and held her hand, she was gone. I heard a loud crashing sound coming from the opposite direction. I didn't even look up to see what was happening; my focus was on my sister. Her eyes were wide open. It looked as if she was looking right at me.

I whispered, "I'm so sorry, Katty. I loved you so much, I'm so sorry. I didn't want it to be this way."

I knew I needed to escape, but at the same time I felt some type of way for leaving my sister like that. Spinx came in out of nowhere and lifted me to my feet. I didn't even realize that Rashawn had lost the battle with Fae. He was lying on the bed holding his throat, gasping for air. Blood was squirting through his fingers. Rashawn reached for me to help him and that's when I noticed his throat gaping open. I blew him a kiss and smiled, as he choked on his own blood. Lying next to him was a broken lamp. *That's what made the crashing sound*, I thought.

"Nyse, get your shit. We got to get the fuck out of here before she get up," Spinx said as he exited the room.

Fae was lying on the floor moaning and holding the back of her head. Fragments of the broken lamp were sticking out of her head and neck. I grabbed my bag and followed Spinx. We went down the stairs into the parking garage and ran to his truck. I was about to get in until I felt someone pulling me back. It was Kevin. *What the hell is he doing here*? I thought. I was afraid. I couldn't trust anyone at this point, especially him, not after what his sister did to Kat. I didn't know if he had anything to do with it. I started my performance. I screamed and fought for him to get off of me.

"Nalyse, it's a trick, he set you up. Don't get in that truck," Kevin warned.

"No it was you, you and that bitch Fae. She killed my sister. Why did you let her do that? Why Kevin? What did she ever do to you?" I was losing it. My true emotions were coming out. I couldn't help it; that was my sister.

"Nyse, you got to believe me, this nigga was going to have you and Rashawn killed tonight. He set a meeting up with Fae a few days ago to plan everything out. I have no idea how your sister got involved, and believe me, I'm sorry that she did. I liked Kat, she was real cool peoples. I'm just happy that you're all right." He tried to hug me, but I pulled away. I guess he didn't know what was really going on, because every word he'd said was what I told Fae to tell him.

"Kevin, you didn't answer my question, what are you doing here?"

"To get you out of here, so Fae could handle her business. I didn't want you to witness any of this. When she told me their plan we set up our own to get rid of them. Especially Rashawn, I found out that he put a $250,000 bounty on my head. He never intended to show up at the shipment it was all a set up."

Spinx got out of the truck and walked slowly around to the

back. He pulled a gun out aiming it at Kevin. "Where the fuck is my brother, nigga? What the fuck did you do with Spade? I know you picked him up the night you set me up."

"No, darling, he didn't set you up, I did." I walked up to Spinx slowly. The look on his face was priceless.

Kevin smiled coolly. "As for your brother, ask your boys, they're the ones who blew up my truck."

Spinx looked confused and hurt. "Nyse, baby, no… not you, Oh my God, not you, Nyse. Why? For this Nigga? You set me up for this piece of shit?"

Spinx raised his gun and aimed it at Kevin, but he would never get a chance to pull the trigger. Fae fired a shot, hitting him in the shoulder. He fell up against the truck.

"Fae! What the fuck is up? Shit, you fucking shot me. Shoot that deceitful bitch; I knew I should have listened to you." He leaned up against his truck. "What the fuck is this nigga talking about? You know what happened to my brother?" Spinx said.

Fae put the barrel to her head like she was thinking. Then she said, "Oh yeah, I remember, you are about to meet him now." She shoved the gun into his mouth and pulled the trigger. "Tell him I said hello." She laughed.

I was thrilled at the sight of Spinx's brain matter splattered against the truck. Then Fae walked up to me and put the gun to my head and everything fell silent. She had a demonic look in her eyes.

Kevin yelled, "Fae, put the fucking gun down."

I kept my eyes glued on Fae. I forced a smile on my face, took a deep breath and said, "Damn, Fae…why the head? You know Queen Kat would want to look fabulous at her final viewing. You know Congo Funeral Home is gonna have a hard time fixing that up." I faked a few laughs and Fae joined in.

She winked at me and smiled. "You are definitely my type of bitch, Nyse."

Kevin had a puzzled look on his face. "I don't know what the fuck y'all are up to, but I know what, Fae you better get this shit cleaned up." He put his arm around me. "We definitely need to talk, but didn't I tell you I would handle our problems."

Little did he know I had handled my own problems and a new one had formed, by the name of Fae.

He held my hand and led me to the car. I looked back at Fae and she was pouring liquid acid on Spinx. You could see smoke rising from his body. For a minute we made eye contact. She beamed with pride when she looked at me. I nodded my head at her. *That's right; you keep on thinking everything is all good,* I thought. This shit was far from over. She'd deceived me, and just like everyone else she had a weakness. His name was Kevin. I had to do it... not just for me but for Kat.

Cartel Publications Order Form
www.thecartelpublications.com

Titles	***Select The Novels You Want Below***	***Fee***
Shyt List	________________	$15.00
Pitbulls In A Skirt	________________	$15.00
Victoria's Secret	________________	$15.00
Poison	________________	$15.00
Hell Razor Honeys	________________	$15.00
A Hustler's Son 2	________________	$15.00
Black And Ugly As Ever	________________	$15.00

Please add $2.00 per book for shipping and handling.
Total: $__________

Mailing Address
The Cartel Publications * P.O. Box 486 * Owings Mills * MD * 21117

Name: ______________________

Address: ______________________

City/State: ______________________

Contact #: ______________________

Email: ______________________

Special Note:
Please allow 5-7 business days for delivery. The Cartel is not responsible for prison orders rejected. **We accept stamps**.

THE CARTEL COLLECTION

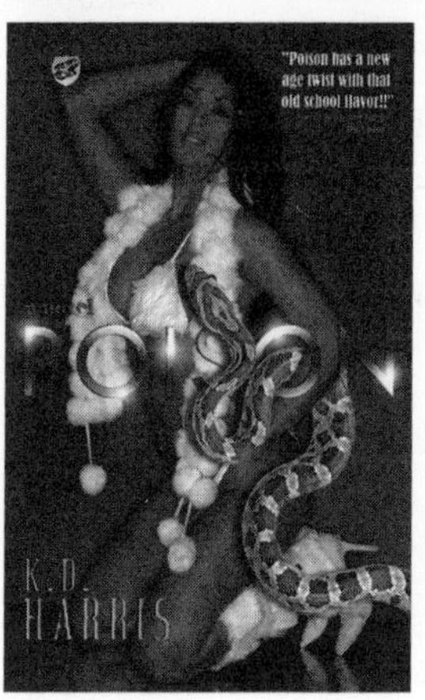